Robert Bage

JAMES WALLACE

in three volumes
Vol. II

Garland Publishing, Inc.
New York & London   *1979*

Bibliographical note:
This facsimile has been made from a copy in
the University of Chicago Library.

*The volumes in this series are printed on acid-free,
250-year-life paper.*

Library of Congress Cataloging in Publication Data

Bage, Robert, 1728–1801.
James Wallace.

(The Novel, 1720–1805)
Reprint of the 1788 ed. printed for W. Lane, London.
I. Title. II. Series.
PZ3.B147Jam   1979   [PR4049.B5]   823'.6   78-60847
ISBN 0-8240-3660-3

Printed in the United States of America

THE
NOVEL
1720–1805

A GARLAND SERIES

selected by
Ronald Paulson
Yale University

THE NOVEL: 1720–1805

1. François de Salignac de la Mothe Fénelon. *The Adventures of Telemachus.*

2. Pierre Carlet de Chamblain de Marivaux. *Le Paysan Parvenu: or, the Fortunate Peasant.*

3. Pierre Carlet de Chamblain de Marivaux. *The Virtuous Orphan or, the Life of Marianne, Countess of* * * * * *

4. Eliza Haywood. *The History of Miss Betsy Thoughtless.*

5. Charles Johnstone. *Chrysal: or, The Adventures of a Guinea.*

6. Henry Brooke. *The Fool of Quality.*

7. Henry Mackenzie. *Julia de Roubigné.*

8. Robert Bage. *Mount Henneth.*

9. Robert Bage. *Barham Downs.*

10. Robert Bage. *The Fair Syrian.*

11. Robert Bage. *James Wallace.*

12. Robert Bage. *Man As He Is.*

13. Robert Bage. *Hermsprong; or, Man As He Is Not.*

14. William Godwin. *Fleetwood: or, The New Man of Feeling.*

15. Thomas Holcroft. *Memoirs of Bryan Perdue.*

JAMES WALLACE,

A NOVEL,

BY THE AUTHOR OF

MOUNT-HENNETH, BARHAM-DOWNS,

AND

THE FAIR SYRIAN.

———————

IN THREE VOLUMES,

———————

VOL II.

LONDON:

Printed for WILLIAM LANE, Leadenhall-Street.

M DCC LXXXVIII.

JAMES WALLACE.

Box, Dec. 20, 1787.

I Acknowledge, dear Mifs Lamounde, that Mifs Thurl is amiable and engaging; and, but for a little jealoufy, I fhould rejoice at your acquifition of fo agreeable a friend: It feems to me alfo that you have an engaging fervant, of whom, if he continues to excite your notice, I fhall be glad to hear. I promifed in my laft an account of Mafter Moreton, fon of Sir Everard, from whom I

have derived one good at leaft, the honour
and pleafure of your friendfhip; for my
prudent Father (fo Mr. Edwards permits
me to call him) not being certain that
the confequence of introducing an un-
bridled young man to a very filly young
woman would be to his liking, fent me
to Mrs. Scott's boarding-fchool, to be out
of the way. This provident intention
was fruftrated by an illnefs of Mrs. Edwards, which required my return, and,
before fhe was well recovered, Mr. Edwards himfelf fell ill. I was of neceffity,
therefore one of the family, and an acquaintance commenced of courfe.

You may probably fuppofe, Mr. Edwards would fortify me with admonition
proper to prevent the connexion he feared.
No; he knew young women better. He
contented himfelf, therefore, with keeping
a tolerable watchful eye over us, without
himfelf putting into our heads what poffibly might not elfe come there.

It

It was a confiderable time before Mr. Moreton took any notice of me, more than common politenefs demanded. My Father loft his fear, and confequently his caution. I played upon the forte-piano; Mr. Moreton was a violinift. Mr. Edwards, glad that his pupil could fpend his hours of recreation fo laudably, promoted our little concerts, and, after a time, left us to perform them by ourfelves.

Mr. Moreton could, whenever he thought it neceffary, behave with the moft infinuating fweetnefs, affume an uncommon tendernefs in his manner, and be all attention to pleafe. I fuppofe thefe things captivate the hearts of moft filly, inexperienced girls like me. He was handfome alfo, had a fine tafte in drefs, was eloquent, of a moft agreeable vivacity, and did not feem to want generofity, and even benevolence. Do I fucceed, my dear Mifs Lamounde, in making an apology for my own weaknefs ? Or is it neceffary to add the vanity that muft arife in fuch a

poor,

poor, forlorn, young creature as I was, on the view of fo fplendid an eftablifhment?

Mr. Moreton had declared himfelf, or rather, had faid and done a thoufand pretty little things that fuperfeded the neceffity of a declaration. I underftood him to be a fincere, an honourable, lover ; for what girl of eighteen dreams of deceit?

But there was a duplicity in the fecret conduct of this bufinefs I did not approve. In the prefence of Mr. and Mrs. Edwards, our words and looks were guarded with uncommon care. Mr. Moreton convinced me, that the confequence of the difcovery of our connexion would be immediate banifhment from all he held dear in life. He knew Mr. Edwards would think it a point of honour to communicate it to his Father ; and he knew the avarice and ambition of his Father too well to flatter himfelf with any immediate hope. I fighed, for I was in love ; I acquiefced, for I was weak ;

but

but the practice of deceit hung heavy on me, and many a pillow did I wet with my tears.

These tears first betrayed me. Mr. Edwards saw my uneasiness, guessed the cause, and communicated the suspicion to Mr. Edwards. Suspicion once awake, all was soon discovered: I was sent to a friend's at a distance, and became for a-while the object of my Father's anger. To confess the truth, my dear Miss La-mounde, he was for a time the object of mine; for such is the nature of love, and probably other passions, that whosoever crosses them, though his reasons were the dictates of eternal truth, becomes another being, an odious being; and affection, reverence, esteem, are all absorbed by this pitiful passion of love.

So, to my everlasting shame I own, so it was with me; and the individual that had protected me, when deprived of all natural protection, whom I adored, and

who

who was intitled to a gratitude that ought to have known no end or limit, now ceafed to excite it. Thanks to the Father of mercies, this ignominous ftate of mind was of fhort duration; reflection prevailed by degrees, and fhewed me the errors of my heart: Not that I did not ftill love, ftill figh; but in proportion as my reafon convinced me I had lefs to hope, I acquired more refignation. I wrote to my Father with tears of penitence; I confeffed my fault with bitter reproaches. In return I had a letter of true affection, and full forgivenefs; I was almoft at eafe.

Mr. Moreton had conjectured truly, that Mr. Edwards would not hefitate to convey this difagreeable affair to Sir Everard. He received an anfwer of thanks and acknowledgement, and his fon a letter full of anger and reproof, with a peremptory command to return home. The young gentleman was not willing to obey any commands but thofe of love,

and

and abfolutely refufed obedience. Mr.
Edwards foothed, reafoned, and remon-
ftrated, in vain. Mr. Moreton was fullen
and filent, except when he broke out
into reproaches for, what he called, Mr.
Edwards's unneceffary and officious inter-
ference. At length Mr. Edwards affumed
the ftern authority of a preceptor, and
informed him he had not a houfe at the
fervice of young men who had loft felf-
government: It was not, however, till
he faw a meffenger ready to depart for his
Father's that his mind could be fubdued.
Poor youth! he pleaded hard for one
interview; but there lives not a more re-
folved man than Mr. Edwards, when his
refolutions are formed by rectitude.

After his departure I was fent for home,
and became again the child of affection;
nay, I think, they loved me even better
than before my deviation from the paths
of propriety. Pity, probably, added
ftrength to affection: It was, however, a
fettled maxim never to introduce the

fubject,

ſubject, nor mention Mr. Moreton's name, and a full year has paſſed away without the leaſt intelligence concerning him.

I try to excuſe him! I had, perhaps, better try to forget. Adieu, my fair friend. Love me not the leſs for the weakneſs of a——woman.

PAULINA EDWARDS.

MISS   LAMOUNDE,

T O

MISS   EDWARDS.

Kirkham, Dec. 27, 1787.

YES, my dear; perhaps it would be better to try to forget, and better ſtill to ſucceed in the endeavour. Though this is a changeable world, there are things in it of more ſtability than young mens vows; and the grand tour, which your lover is now taking by way of penance,

is

is a wonderful deſtroyer of firſt loves. I
came very honeſtly by this ſecret of the
tour ; my brother is abroad ; they met
upon the road, and are now at Paris together. My dear Paulina, exert yourſelf
in the recovery of your former tone of
mind, and do not depend upon *love* for
happineſs.

I am now upon a viſit to Miſs Thurl.
You deſire a farther acquaintance with
this amiable lady ; and you deſire alſo
more anecdote concerning my ſervant
Wallace ; theſe deſires are very reaſonable,
Paulina ; young women would ſcarcely
ever form any other, were it not for ——
men. I ſhall beſt gratify them by a little
hiſtory of our words and works.

As I had given my friend notice of my
coming, the young 'ſquire was ready to
hand me out, and, by way of welcome,
ſaluted me with a hearty ſmack : I bluſh-
ed. " Brother, ſays Miſs Thurl, Miſs
Lamounde's ſtay here will be very ſhort,
if ſhe is to be expoſed to ſuch rudeneſs."
B 5   " Rudeneſs !

" Rudenefs ! anfwers the 'fquire ; why there now, women be always in the wrong. It's out of pure kindnefs ; befides, you never barred kiffing."

" We bar it now then."

" Well—fince you be fo frumpifh and dainty, I'll fit you." — I was introduced to the old 'fquire and his lady ; he laid up with the gout, fhe with an afthma ; they feldom come down ftairs.

" I'm glad to fee you, Mifs Lamounde, fays the old gentleman, in a frank, hearty way, you're kindly welcome.   Lord ! how the world wags ! I remember calling upon your Father for his vote, when you were a child in frocks.   How the world wags ! It is but a day fince, and fee how you're grown ! Well ! and how does your uncle Paul ? gruff old Paul? He was againft us, but an honeft man for all that : It's pity he fhould be a whig ; he muft grow old now, Mifs Lamounde—and I

grow

grow old—Time, with his ſtealing ſteps, hath clawed me in his clutch, as the old ſong ſays : And this curſed gout; but it is what we muſt all come to. Nothing ſo ſure as death and taxes."

" Never talk of dying, Father, ſays the young 'ſquire; it's melancholy, and Miſs came here to be merry."

" Good, Havelley, good. Hang ſorrow, and caſt away care, as the poet ſays. It's very good of you, Miſs Lamounde, to come and ſee Caroline; ſhe's moped, for we han't a deal of company o'late. Havelley don't fancy the neighbouring gentry; for why? He's up to any thing manly; but the young gentlemen of this age be all women ! What dreſſing, and powdering, and puffing ! Lord ! how they ſhiver at a bit o'froſt !"

The ceremony of introduction being over, my agreeable friend carried me to my apartments to dreſs; and as I came

B 6   alone

alone in a hired chaife, afked me if I was afraid of eating them up, that I brought with me neither man-fervant, nor maid-fervant?

" No, my dear, I anfwered; it was becaufe I did not imagine Mr. Wallace would be an agreeable object to Mr. Havelley; and befides, he is at prefent en-engaged in a bufinefs that it would be cruelty to take him from. As to a maid, why you muft know I have only, as the lawyers fay, an undecided moiety of one, my aunt and I being joint tenants."

" Pretty, fays Mifs Thurl, that muft now and then make fome agreeable confufion; œconomy—I fuppofe ?"

" Œconomy in my aunt, in my uncle a peculiarity. He thinks every additional fervant an additional plague. Leave, fays he to me one day, leave, Judith, thefe fplendid plagues to the rich and great. I would fooner undertake to govern the
Chickefaws,

Chickesaws, than a house of well-dressed
gentleman and lady servants."

" Your uncle is right, my dear ; we
have only sixteen, and a housekeeper, and
we have three factions that fill the state
with troubles. Upon my brother's account there was no necessity for leaving the
spirited Mr. Wallace behind. My brother bears no malice. You have great
obligations to him I find ; but such is the
pride and ingratitude of beauty, I question
if you will acknowledge them. Unknown to me he has invited half a score
of *his own* friends, purely to make you
merry."

" Wisdom, saith I, endureth all things."

" I hope then, says she, it will be able
to endure my cousin, Sir Antony Havelley, a baronet of moderate fortune,
and immoderate talents. He is an old,
grave gentleman, of thirty, enamoured
of all the out of the way things in nature,

nice

nice and fplendid in apparel, exact in his
ceremonials, delicate, nervous, and apt to
be difordered by an Eaft-wind.   Take
care of your heart."

The firft week we fpent in receiving a
rich fucceffion of vifitants.   We eat and
drank, talked of London, Liverpool, and
lace, and *confolidated* our fociety with
quadrille ; but pleafure endureth not for
ever.   With the abfence of company
came a vacuity, which the young 'fquire
knew not how to fill up.   Love was in-
terdicted, and all the rich fund of manual
wit and humour :. It was a condition not
to be borne ; and, to get rid of it, the
'fquire was determined to fetch his dear
friend, Jack Cornbury, to entertain us
with the cutler's wheel, and the growling
of dogs about a bone.

In his abfence arrived the valet de
chambre of Sir Antony Havelley, to announce the approach of his mafter, to
prepare his apartments, and arrange his
toilette.

" It

" It is a lovely morning, my dear, says Mifs Thurl; the fun and the birds invite us, a thoufand flowers are wafting their fweetnefs on the defart air, and we know not when we can again enjoy an uninterrupted walk." I accepted the propofal with pleafure. In the midft of our walk, my fair friend reminded me that I had promifed her fome anecdotes concerning my fervant Wallace, whom fhe was pleafed to call her favourite. I promifed the fame to you, my Paulina, and I now write what I faid to Mifs Thurl on the fubject.

It is difficult to explain the odd way we are in with him. Through the whole of his words and actions, it was impoffible not to obferve a fomething that denoted he was now below his proper fituation; yet he gave himfelf no airs, affumed no pride, claimed no exemption. Whatfoever queftions were afked him, he anfwered with extreme modefty, and in few words; but with an intelligence that invited us to afk them frequently. In
fhort,

fhort, a certain degree of freedom and familiarity took place imperceptibly. We faw him perform his little offices without reflecting they did not belong to him; and when we had not company, drew him into converfation without reflecting he had thefe little offices to perform.

My uncle, by the aid of contracted eye-brows, and fome afperity of language, conceals a kind and benevolent heart. He feldom fpeaks to pleafe, and ftill more feldom acts to offend. He likes to talk notwithftanding, and will often take the fide of abfurdity for the fake of puzzling my aunt and me. One day at dinner he got deep into a labyrinth, yet carried it fo triumphantly, that my aunt appealed to Mr. Wallace. He gave not his own opinion, but mentioned an elegant author who had wrote on the fubject, and from whom he gave two or three quotations.

" So, Sir—fays my uncle—you are one of thofe who decide by authority."

" If

" If the authority is good, Sir."

" There is no good authority but reafon ; names are nothing.   Support your
caufe from your own bottom, fince you
have undertaken it, and leave quotations
to pedants.   It was impoffible for a man
to fpeak with greater modefty; but the
fubject from being fimple became learned,
and my uncle feemed bent upon trying
the extent of Mr. Wallace's knowledge.
It appeared that he was acquainted with
French and Latin.   At length, my uncle
dropping the argument, and his knife and
fork with it, looked full in Wallace's face,
and faid, with an emphafis, Young man,
who are you ?

Mr. Wallace anfwered only by a look
of furprife.

That your education is fuperior to your
condition, fays my uncle, is evident.   You
have concealments therefore, and concealments breed fufpicion.   How do we know
for

for what kind of folly you may now be doing penance? Errors of youth are pardonable; but, whilst you dare not be ingenuous, how dare we confide?

I thought this very harsh in my uncle; was it not?

Mr. Wallace, however, with a pleasing placid smile, said, pardon me, Sir, the charge against me is rather too heavily laid. I know not why I should be thought anxious to conceal, where I do not remember to have been interrogated. If I have been unfortunate, I have no right with impertinent loquacity, to intrude the knowledge of my misfortunes upon others; and it would be folly to advance a claim upon compassion, which, if allowed, might render an easy situation irksome. Permit me to say, I feel the value of my present situation sensibly: I have in it a satisfaction and content which I never remember to have had before. I ought to be cautious how I put it to the risque.

" You

" You were born then in a fuperior rank of life; you are of family, perhaps."

" Do not let me miflead you, Sir; I know nothing of my family. I never was in affluence, confequently have no right to murmur at the want of wealth. My education is accident: That I have been in better fituations (others will call them better, though I do not) is more a deviation from the common occurrences of life, than to be what I am."

A lady, who called herfelf Wallace, attended only by one maid, came in the dufk of the evening to the houfe of Mr. Holman, an apothecary, at Allington, in this county, and, after a conference with Mr. Holman, took up her refidence for a time; fhe was in the laft month of pregnancy, and in due time was brought to bed of me. She ftaid her month, and then went away, leaving me behind. It muft be confeffed, that Mr. Holman has always been much upon the referve whenever the

fubject

subject has been touched; but his account is, that the lady never communicated her family; that she gave him a little money for my maintenance, and a small packet well sealed; that she obtained a promise from him, nay an oath, that he would preserve this packet so sealed six years; that if in that time he did not see or hear from her, the contents of the packet would explain all the mystery, restore me to my relations, and procure him a proper return for his kindness.

This packet Mr. Holman carefully locked up in his study amongst his most valued papers. Unfortunately, about the middle of the fifth year, a fire broke out in his study, and consumed this packet with other papers of value; and as my mother has not since been heard of, there cannot well be a smaller probability than that I should ever come to the knowledge of my family; nor if I could, is the probability much greater that I should be benefited by it.

Mr.

Mr. Wallace then acquainted us of his having been apprenticed to a lawyer, and of a number of fmall misfortunes which had fince befallen him ; but which at pre-fent I have not time to communicate. He concluded, with expreffing a hope, that as he claimed no confideration from the obfcurity of his birth, it would not operate in our minds againft him.

" That, fays my uncle, would be un-juft ; but I muft wonder to fee a young man of talents with fo little ambition."

" Why fhould I nourifh a paffion, Sir, from which I have hitherto reaped only delufion. It is in your family alone I have met with kindnefs, protection, and con-tent. Thefe valuable bleffings you will not wonder that I endeavour to render as permanent as I can."

After this elucidation, my dear Paulina, my uncle did treat him with more confi-deration, though he fometimes ftrove to

hide

hide it. My aunt changed her tone to greater foftnefs, and now and then ventured an encomium. For my part, as I never treated him much *en maitreſſe*, I had not the appearance of any confiderable change; yet I know not how it is—I do feel a difference: I reverence him more I think. It is an odd term, my dear, to be applied to a footman; but I owe it lefs, I believe, to his unfortunate tale, than to fome other circumftances which I am going to mention.

I was reading one afternoon in the parlour alone, and wanting fomething, rang the bell. Being much engaged in a tender tale, I did not at firft perceive Mr. Wallace's entrance: When I did, his fine face was all in a glow; he trembled, and had every mark of perturbation about him.

"What is the matter, fays I; you feem ruffled?"

"I

"I have been upon the dock, Madam, for my mafter, and have feen a failor fall into the water, and drowned by the contention to fave him. The alarm had reached his wife, who ran with a child in her arms, and fainted upon the corpfe; they were carried home fenfelefs together. I followed amongft a crowd, none of which feemed able to comfort or relieve. It feemed, indeed, a hopelefs bufinefs. When fhe recovered I endeavoured it. The little money I had about me, I gave her for prefent fupport. She thanked me, but comfort, fhe faid, could never be hers on this fide the grave. Don't defpair, fays I, you will be largely affifted; the merchants of Liverpool are too generous to let a failor's wife want. No, fays fhe, I fhall not want whi.ft I live; but I am dying of an incurable cancer, and what will become of my fix poor orphans? Oh! Madam, continues Mr. Wallace — whilft you are weeping the fictitious diftreffes of a Catharine did you but know what real calamities are around you!"

There

There was, my dear Paulina, fomething fo humble in Mr. Wallace's looks when he faid this, it was fo totally unmixed, with any air, or any pertnefs of manner, that, though the expreffion feemed to convey a reproach, it never entered my head to be angry.   I am fcarcely able, to develope the nature of my emotion; but fts immediate effect was a kind of inftinct ive pulling out my purfe, and prefenting it to him.

He drew back: "No, Madam, fays he, though I wifh to excite your benevolence, for I wifh to increafe your happinefs, I dare not be your almoner."

"Why, Mr. Wallace?"

"Becaufe to be driven from your fervice would, in my apprehenfion, be the greateft of misfortunes; and I dare not place myfelf in a ftate of poffible fufpicion."

"Mr.

" Mr. Wallace, fays I, take it without fear; I cannot fufpect."

" On this occafion, Madam, you will have the goodnefs to excufe me. Your benevolence will not, I am perfuaded, be neceffary here; nor have I exhaufted the liberality of your brother."

" Promife me then you will apply to me, whenever you think any future neceffity arifes there or elfewhere."

He bowed, and was half a minute filent. " If I might prefume, fays he, but — I dread your anger ———."

" Speak without fear, Mr. Wallace; if my anger could be excited by your goodnefs, it would ill deferve to be dreaded."

" I could point out to you the unmerited diftrefs of two very deferving fifters, who had their little fortunes of a thoufand pounds each in the hands of an uncle. This uncle went off yefterday, and will become a bankrupt. The young ladies are newly arrived at Liverpool. Having loft Father and Mother, they came to live with this their neareft relation. The ftroke has come fo fuddenly upon them, that they are overwhelmed with affliction. It is not relief they have occafion for, it is kindnefs, it is confolation. They have not had time for want ———."

" So then, fays I, you are not content with benevolence in the form of money ?"

" No, fays he (a fine glow overfpreading his face) I would have it in the form of an angel." On faying this he retired haftily.

I muft confefs, my dear Paulina, per-haps to my fhame, that the doctrine of perfonal acquaintance with diftrefs was new to me, and not perfectly agreeable either to my pride or inclination ; yet I

know

know not how it was : I could not reft
till I had executed the will of this my
extraordinary inftructor. The event was
happy; the young ladies were confoled,
and I had my reward in a great number
of new and agreeable fenfations : I
thanked Mr. Wallace for having procured
them. He bowed, and faid, he believed
the greateft of human pleafures was procured by a habit of active and perfonal
benevolence, and he wifhed me the greateft
of human pleafures.

A few days before I left home, I heard
a female voice at the kitchen door, faying
to Sally, my half maid, " Pray tell him
my name is Dorrington, and I hope he
will have the goodnefs to let me fee him
as foon as poffible; but why fhould I
doubt his goodnefs, who have felt its
effects fo largely; God blefs him where-
ever he goes.

I fuppofe, Paulina, you know fomething of female curiofity. I rang for
Sally.

Sally. " What woman was it you were talking to ?"

" One of Mr. Wallace's trollops, I ſuppoſe, ſays ſhe; he has them calling every now and then."

" Why do you give her ſo coarſe a title ?"

" Becauſe, Madam, ſhe looks for all the world like them there creatures, ſo ſhabby fine."

" She did not talk like one. This has the appearance of ſpite to Wallace: I ſuppoſe he is not in your favour."

" No, nor never will while he's ſo proud. What if he does not wear a li-very ? that's your goodneſs more than his deſert; but, indeed, Madam, he's quite ſpoiled above ſtairs."

" This is new language, Sally."

" Nay,

" Náy, Me'm, I don't mean for to offend you; for I fees nothing but good-nature from you to every body, fo no wonder he comes in for his fhare; but Madam Lamounde did not ufe to be fo gentle, and I'm fure fhe could not fpeak kinder to him if he was her own fon, and he's young enough."

" Let me hear nothing difrefpectful of my aunt."

" Poor farvants are fnubbed, let 'em fpeak truth ever fo much; but you'll fee one day."

What I fhall fee one day, I don't know; but, I think, I do perceive a change in my aunt : It is, however, for the better.

When I faid this to Mifs Thurl, Pau-lina, fhe faid, in her manner—I wifh you faw her manner—" And pray, my dear, don't you feel—as it were—fome flight matter of change in yourfelf?"

C 3   " Yes,

" Yes, Mifs Thurl, I have changed my manner of thinking in feveral refpects; I have lefs pride I hope, lefs vanity, and more compaffion."

" That's well, fays fhe; but who is Mrs. Dorrington ?"

I afked the queftion of Mr. Wallace, who told me fhe was once a Mifs Dean, of Cambridge, the daughter of a fhop-keeper, poor, but proud. Her careful Mother had brought her up to drefs, to vifit early, that, as foon as poffible, fhe might get rid of that retiring modefty, the foolifh poets of the laft age praifed fo much, and to make an appearance, the firft ftudy of the prefent age.

The pretty Mifs Dean, it feems, cap-tivated Mr. Godfrey Dorrington, a Cam-bridge fcholar, of nineteen. She was too tender-hearted to kill the youth who loved her. Her Father was confulted, who ge-neroufly gave his confent to their union, and furnifhed them out for Gretna-Green.

Godfrey

Godfrey was an orphan, and under the guardianſhip of his uncle, a bachelor, who lived in Norfolk, and whoſe heir he was. To this uncle he wrote from Gretna - Green for money and pardon. Godfrey's own fortune was two thouſand pounds ; and when he arrived at Cambridge, he found Mr. Bond, an attorney, there, ready to pay him this fortune, and to aſſure him, that he had loſt for ever his uncle's affection, and eight hundred pounds a year.

But he might relent, and, upon the ſtrength of this poſſibility, this young couple took a ſmall country-houſe, and ſet off with a daſh. No deity intervening they were ſoon undone, and Godfrey had no other expedient than to take orders. He removed from curacy to curacy with a wife and three children, and at length ſettled at Liverpool on a curacy of fifty pounds a year. Having enjoyed this eſtabliſhment ſix months, an intermitting fever incapacitated him for duty. The good rector bore it patiently a whole

month,

month, and then difmiffed him. Since
this he has lived upon air, and making
ghofts and murders for one of our news-
papers. In this difmal fituation, he had
the confoling intelligence that his uncle
was dead, and had bequeathed him ——
one fhilling !

" My acquaintance with him, fays
Mr. Wallace, began at the bookfeller's-
fhop. I perceived he had learning and
genius, and I never could look upon his
poor, emaciated figure, without a pang;
but when, upon a particular occafion, I
was induced to call at his houfe, and found
an elegant woman, three pretty female
children, hunger, rags, and defpair.——
Good God ! Madam, what heart could
ftand it !"

" Was 1 fo funk in your efteem, Mr.
Wallace, that you chofe not to have recourfe to me ?"

" Madam !

" Madam !—Miſs Lamounde !— for God's ſake !—ſunk in *my* eſteem, Madam ! — But you know how preſumptuous I have lately been : However, as all I had, and all Mr. James Lamounde gave me, is gone, I muſt ſoon have had recourſe to your goodneſs ; but my hopes for my new friend is not confined to mere acts of charity. From certain things that fell in converſation, I ſuſpect Mr. Godfrey Dorrington is heir to all his uncle's real property, notwithſtanding the will. It would be tedious to you, Madam, to ſpeak of the nature of modern tenures, and what forms are neceſſary to turn them out of the legal channel. Theſe forms, I think, have not been complied with. I have conſulted Mr. Wilſon, your attorney, whoſe ſkill and integrity are well known : He has wrote to council ; enquiries have been made, and the aſpect is very promiſing : But we want a man of weight to countenance us ; a man not deficient in ſpirit, in purſe, or in generoſity ; ſuch a one as my maſter."

" I

" I wish you had him."

" I don't despair of it, if you will have the goodness to introduce the subject, when there is leisure to pursue it." I promised.

We supped without company, and my uncle seeming to be in a good-humoured mood, I began, by saying to Wallace, " A Mrs. Dorrington, a very pretty woman they say, called upon you this afternoon, Mr. James: I doubt you are not punctual to your appointments, to give the lady this trouble; but, though she was impatient, she was secret; she would not impart an Iota of her business."

" Oh! says my aunt, that's the trollop that Sally told me of: I desire to know who she is, and what she is."

" Nay, Rebecca, says my uncle, that is too much to desire; if the lady is delicate, the gentleman ought to be discreet."

" Don't

" Don't tell me, brother, every mafter ought to infpect the conduct of his domeftics. If there is any bad doings, don't the reputation of the houfe fuffer? Who is the trollop, I fay?"

" A poor gentlewoman, Madam, in diftrefs."

" What have you to do with them?"

" Affift them, Madam, if I could."

" Now, I think, you fhould leave it to thofe that are richer."

" Moft willingly, Madam, if the rich would undertake it; but, as my miftrefs very juftly obferves, domeftics ought always to be under a mafter's eye; and I fhall be happy if you will permit me to explain my connexion with Mrs. Dorrington. If I have been wrong, I fhall be benefited by your reproof; if right, by your advice."

My

My uncle not denying, Wallace told the tale, my dear Paulina, with fo pretty a mixture of the pathetic, that my uncle had fome difficulty to preferve the ftoic compofure of his face. When the ftory ended, he contracted his brow into a frown, and faid——" And fo, Sir, you would really have me undertake the caufe of thefe filly people ?"

" I own I wifh it, Sir."

" To rob folly of its proper reward; you mention the man's genius and learning : Sir, they are his peculiar condemnation. Pretty qualities, to wafte in idlenefs and vanities !"

" Their folly has been great, Sir; fo has been their punifhment. For a few cups of honey, they have long drank the waters of bitternefs. The innocent children too, Sir —— !"

" Are

" Are punished for the sins of their Fathers. That is a divine ordinance, and you would counteract it."

" I would, indeed, Sir."

" When you go about to divert the ordinary course of human affairs, how do you know but you are creating more future evil, than you are doing present good ? You remember Zadig."

" The conduct of an angel, who can see into futurity, may be directed with certainty to the greatest good. Men can only be guided by what they know. I am sure, Sir, it is no maxim of yours, that no one ought to attempt a probable and proximate good, for fear of producing a remote and improbable evil."

" No, Sir—but man is an ass—these remote and improbable evils are upon his right-hand and upon his left, whilst the fool, guided by passion or prejudice, will only look strait forward."

" Passion,

" Paſſion, Sir, and prejudice, I hope, are not the general guides to charity, com-paſſion, and benevolence."

" I hate the cant of benevolence ; books are full of it ; it fills our mouth, and ſometimes gets as far as the eye, but never reaches the heart."

" Not never, Sir."

" What is it at beſt, but the oſtentation of vanity ?"

" Not at *beſt*, Sir ; that can hardly be allowed to be the motive of a man, who is pleaſed to do good, and pleaſed to con-ceal it."

" If there be any ſuch, the man is aſhamed of his folly, perhaps."

" There are ſentiments, Sir, which iſſue from the mouth, and are contradicted by the feelings of the heart. Will you have
the

the goodnefs to pardon me, Sir, if I fufpect your affumed principles ill agree
with your practice ?"

" Practice, Sir ! Does any man accufe
me of thefe milky doings ?"

" Some men, Sir, and fome women:
If all gratitude were as ftrong as Mrs.
Calthorpe's, you would not be able to
do good by ftealth."

" Humph ! fays my uncle—ftopping
for a minute : But, continues he, Mrs.
Calthorpe was as handfome as Mrs. Dorrington, perhaps. My commiferation
might be excited by beauty ; fo may
yours."

" More fhame for him then, fays my
aunt."

" I am not infenfible to beauty, Sir,
replied Wallace ; nor when I fee benefi-
cent effects, am I folicitous to trace them

to

to their caufes.   Pride performs great
things, and vanity good ones; had they
no other operation, who would not call
them virtues ?"

" In confequence, you have never taken
the trouble to fcrutinize your own motives ; a fure way to avoid the mortification of finding under what defpicable
commander you have acted."

" Not defpicable, Sir, when he leads
me on to victory."

" Victory !"

" Over avarice, perhaps ; felf-love, or
indolence ; perhaps, over himfelf."

" Well, Sir—you are very allegorical
and poetical ; and I am a plain, blunt, old
fellow, juft able to fpell common fenfe."

" I fear I have been impertinent, Sir,
and humbly beg pardon."

                              " No—

" No—I invited you to the conteſt, and you have ſuſtained it well ; not that. your arguments are profound, but they are pretty. I dare ſay Judith thinks them ſo, and my ſiſter Rebecca."

' I confeſs I do, replies I."

" Now I don't, ſays my aunt."

" Well, Sir—I will confider the matter, as ſoon as I can ſtrip it of your damned tropes and figures. To-morrow, perhaps, if I don't find myſelf too much a fool for it, I may call in with you at Wilſon's, or Dorrington's." — Wallace, his eyes ſparkling with gratitude, finiſhed his buſineſs, for ſupper was now over, and withdrew.

" I believe, ſays my uncle, after a minute's ſilence, there never was a houſe ſo fitted up with a footman."

. . . . . .

Pox take the puppy ! I know now he will plague and fret me into this fooliſh buſineſs ;

nefs; yet won't leave me the comfort of being angry at him.

But I'm fure he fhould not, fays my aunt.

" What the devil, continues my uncle, has a fellow, not worth a groat, to do with thefe exalted notions ?"

" That's what's I fay, brother; he's out of his latitude."

" Ay, and longitude too, Beck; a footman pretend to goodnefs! I hope thou wilt get him difcharged for it."

" Lord! brother, if one fays as you fay, then you go and fay quite the con-trary; I muft few up my mouth, I believe."

" Thy tongue will break the ftitches; but, Judith — I am of opinion, this man fhould be no longer your footman."

" So

" So am I too, uncle ; yet it would be an extraordinary motive to difcharge him for goodnefs."

" If we cannot difcharge, we may tranf-late him. Doft think he might be trufted in the accompting-houfe, Jude ? Dare I make him cafhier ?"

" Can you poffibly fufpect his honefty?"

" Any man's honefty *may* be fufpected. I am an old man, Judith, and have had a great many dealings with this fame ho-nefty. I know the dog to the bottom : Let him be as ftaunch as he will, he will yield, after all his barking, to the fop he moft likes."

" Who deals in trope and figure now, Sir ?"

" Pfhaw ! whofe honefty is it will ftand firm againft his ruling paffion ? The key of my cafh would fleep quietly in Wallace's

lace's pocket, when he was folicited only by common vanities : But you fee the turn the fellow's head has taken ; a weeping Mother, efpecially if fhe was handfome, with half a dozen fupperlefs children, would unlock my bureau, provided he had no money of his own, and off fly my guineas half over the town."

" I think I fhould forgive him, Sir."

" I believe thee ; thy fex has a priviledge to be fools upon all crying occafions."

" Yes — and I know you like us the better for it."

" May be fo."—So ended this dialogue; nor were my uncle's fears vain, for it is certain he did get entangled, and in four days had acquired a tolerable quantity of zeal for the caufe. " I will right the Dorringtons, fays he, if it coft me a thoufand pounds."

Here,

Here, Paulina, Miſs Thurl deſired to know how I approved my uncle's ſcheme of tranſlation.

" I don't know, anſwered I. Certainly I ought not to oppoſe the young man's good ; and yet—I own—I ſhould like as well to keep him where he is ; for I don't know how it is, but I actually feel a ſort of ſuperior eaſe and confidence when he is near me : Is it not odd ?"

" Vaſtly ſo, anſwered Miſs Thurl ; how can you be ſo wicked as to wiſh to prevent his riſing under your uncle's auſpices ?"

" I don't know ; we all prefer our own convenience, I believe."

" Should you rather wiſh him to riſe under the auſpices of your aunt ?"

" My aunt ! Miſs Thurl ?"

" Your aunt, Miſs Lamounde."

" What

" What a fantaſtic idea ?"

" Yes, child, it is ſo — but you'll ſee one day, as Sally ſays."

You ſee, my dear Paulina, what my wild, amiable friend has got in her head ; and ten to one ſhe does not ſpare me in her ſuſpicions. How whimſical it is ? Only think, Paulina.

Adieu,

JUDITH LAMOUNDE.

JAMES LAMOUNDE,

T O

MISS JUDITH LAMOUNDE.

Paris, Jan. 2, 1788.

I HAVE received my dear ſiſter's let- ter, and acknowledge the juſtice of her reflections. There *is* no true pleaſure

in

in the gratification of irregular defires.
I have feen the folly of others, and felt
my own : I am determined to begin to
be wife, and the firft fteps to it are to
return to England, embrace my fifter, and
fall in love with her fair friend, the lovely
Mifs Thurl.

But I fee not the equality of my putting on chains, whilft my fifter who forged
them is free. I thought it the duty of
an indulgent brother to return the obli-
gation ; but, Judith, thy Chriftian name
is againft thee. In vain I have affured
my friend, Mr. Mcreton, that my fifter
is fuperlatively handfome, and witty
enough, and gay and fafhionable enough;
no reafonable man need defire a wife to
be more fo. In vain I have informed
him, that thy name is nothing more than
the remains of an auftere Calvinifm,
that once got into the family blood. —
Still he is unable to conceive my fprightly
fifter, *Judith*, to be any thing but a pre-
cife grace-faying, primitive damfel, with

a brown, unpowdered head of hair, turned up under a round mob. He ſhall ſee. I think, in my laſt, I mentioned the valuable acquaintance we had contracted here with a Monſieur Vauclan. I am now to note a few of its conſequences.

There are gaming tables at Paris, dear Judith, to ſome of which this worthy gentleman did us the honour of an introduction. A young man, ſiſter, who travels for improvement, muſt go where he can find it. We won and loſt, and loſt and won, like gentlemen. One unfortunate night we happened to be ſtripped by two Italians. I loſt——no matter ——.

I awoke next morning with a pain in my head, and another in my heart. I dreſſed, and felt in my pockets the neceſſity of an application to my banker. I drew a draft, and laid it on the table; it encountered Scipio's eyes as he brought in my coffee. " Damn," ſays Scipio.

" What's the matter ?"

" Me

" Me go curfed often, Monfieur San-
fon's——Me not know what comes of de
money !"

" Go once more, Scipio, and I will
get ready my accounts for your infpection.
Scipio departed : I fat down ferioufly
enough to a ferious bufinefs, and when
Scipio returned, had generalized my accounts as under :

		£.	s.	d.
Art. 1ft. Lent Mr. Moreton, at } fundry times - }		1200	0	0
2d. Ditto Monfieur Vauclan		330	0	0
3d. Neceffary expences - -		376	0	0
4th. Unneceffary - - - -		1352	0	0
5th. Loft laft night at Cauffin's		360	0	0
6th. Lent Vauclan there - -		480	0	0
7th. Ditto Moreton - - - -		500	0	0

Damn—fays Scipio—but Scipio trembled—his eyes twinkled—and a tear or
two fell. I could have joined him with
all my heart; but it would have been
adding a woman's folly to a man's. I
endeavoured to bring back Scipio to his

uſual tone, that I might have the benefit of his remarks.

" Well, Scipio, what think you ?"

" Sir—Moſſer—me obſerve when you have ſpent evening of jollity, you have de morning of head-ach. De low ſpirited day always follow de gaming night. — Now, Sir, if you get ſix hours of de pleaſures, you pay wid ſix hours of de pains; and ſo you give away de money for noting."

" Juſt ſo, Scipio."

" Sir — me do love you dearly — but me do not love die of de broken heart."

" Be ſatisfied, Scipio ; I ſee my folly, and have done with it. I will return to England immediately, and ſettle, and grow wiſe, and rich, and croſs, like my uncle."

" Me no like Monſieur Vauclan."

" Nor

" Nor I neither ; but how shall I avoid him the short time I stay ?"

" Ask him pay you, Sir; if he do — good—well ; if he do not, he no come near you. Me tink de debt bad ; me don't know if de oder, Mr. Moreton, very good."

" Why so, Scipio ?"

" He be de what you call de minor. If he do lose life soon, he cannot pay you; if he do lose honour, den he wont."

" Of this, Scipio, I am in no fear."

Whilst we were still upon the subject, in came my two dear friends, and propo-fed a scheme for the day so spirited, so joyous.—Nothing could have been better adapted to try the strength of my reso-lution. " Gentlemen, says I, my pockets are empty."

" Apply

" Apply to thy banker," quoth Vauclan.

" No—I have been there too much—I had juft thought of applying to you."

" Me! fays Moreton; I will pay thee when I am a knight."

" And I, when I have a battoon. At prefent I have not a Louis; *mais diable!* What doft thou talk of? A man of thy fortune, unincumber'd with a Father, what difficulty canft thou have in raifing the coriander feeds. *Parbleu,* I engage to procure thee five thoufand Louis-d'ors in twenty-four hours."

" It would be more agreeable to me if you would chufe to leffen your own debt, rather than increafe mine."

" *Diable!* fays Vauclan, what a plague ails thee to-day?"

" I

" I leave Paris almoft immediately, Mr. Moreton ; I fear I fhall not have the pleafure of your company."

" What damn'd perverfity haft thou got in thy head, Lamounde ? Doft thou not know it is but fix days fince I engaged with Madame Moreau, of the Italian theatre ?"

" Six days more will be a proper time to diffolve it."

" Who, but a fplenetic Englifhman, fays Vauclan, would be fo curfedly peevifh for one night's ill luck ? Come, More-ton—let us leave him to his—enjoyments. Lamounde—we dine at Fruelle's. Adieu."

I was determined to ftay one fortnight more at Paris, and fpend it in cultivating the acquaintance of a few literati here of my own tafte, and in feeing things, a lit-tle more worthy to be feen than thofe frivolous ones upon which I had hitherto

D 3   employed

employed my eyes. I fought no longer the fociety of my dear friends. My dear friends fought not me.

1 had begun to prepare for my return, when one morning the Rev. Mr. Hilliard honoured me with a call. His round, ruddy face was lengthened into an oval; and, throwing his wearied body into a chair, and wiping off the fweat that plentifully bedewed his brow—" Why, fays he, why did I undertake the rafh tafk of bridling the fallies of intemperate youth? There was a time, Mr. Lamounde, when young men had a reverence for age and wifdom. *Sed tempora mutantur.* If I had not the comfort of having faithfully difcharged my duty, I fhould be inconfolable. I admonifhed my pupil daily when I could; but, would you believe it, Mr. Lamounde, in the laft three months I have not feen him three half hours. I underftand too, that you have broke off acquaintance with him. If fo, to whom

fhall

shall I apply to releafe him from thral-
dom. I beg your advice."

" What is the circumftance, Sir ?"

" Sir—it is moft difgraceful ! Taken
for debt ! If not directly releafed, he will
be lodged in the Little Chattelet."

What could I do, dear Judith ? Tho'
Moreton has at prefent the follies of
youth, he is a moft agreeable wild fellow,
and will in time have the virtues of a man.
I could not fee my countryman and friend
confined for the paltry fum of five hundred pounds, fo I accompanied Mr. Hilliard to the houfe of the officer.

Whilft we were in the Fiacre, this Rev.
gentleman continued to lament the calamities of a tutor in woful terms. Once
more he requefted the favour of my advice, for fays he, though a young man,
you have much folidity.

When

" When thefe embarraffments happen, I anfwered, it is ufual for tutors to ftate the matter to the parents or guardians of their pupils, and take their direction."

" But, Sir — our laft accounts from England do teftify, that Sir Everard Moreton is rather in an odd way. He hath had a ftroke, Sir; ftrokes are dangerous. One would not aggravate his malady."

" Nor alienate the mind of the young gentleman at fo critical a time."

" Certainly, Sir. For you muft imagine, Mr. Lamounde, although I am totally devoid of avarice, that I would not have left my *otium cum dignitate*, and become a drudge for mere temporary emolument. I had permanent views ; I had promifes, Sir. I have a fon and daughter, Mr. Lamounde : I have a Father's affections, Sir, a Father's anxiety. If I covet preferment, it is for their fakes."

The

The Fiacre ſtopt; we found Moreton rather more low ſpirited than became a buck, upon ſo trifling an occaſion. He had wrote Vauclan, and received a billet in anſwer: In this Vaulcan curſed his hard fortune; for that, being under the neceſſity of going inſtantly to Verſailles, he could not fly to the relief of his dear friend till after the tedious ſpace of three intire days, and adviſed him to apply to me.

As ſoon as the neceſſary forms were gone through, we departed for my lodgings. Moreton, in ſufficient ſpirits to damn the inſolence of his *taileur,* his *marchand de draps,* and the police; and the tutor reading lectures according to cuſtom, though, it muſt be owned, the mild air of Paris had rather ſoftened their aſperity.

I come now, my dear ſiſter, to the laſt act of our comedy. Mr. Moreton had the goodneſs to ſee his folly, to repent of it, and to prefer my company to Vauclan's almoſt a week. In that time I had

D 5   the

the happiness to convince him he miftook the path of pleafure, and that Monfieur Vauclan was by no means an eligible pre- ceptor. He allowed the truth of all I faid, fwore Vauclan was little better than a fcoundrel, and difappeared the fixth day. He had languifhed, it feems, for the joys at Mr. Couffin's, had met Vauclan there, renewed his intimacy, and thefe, dear friends, were fomewhere enjoying the fnug pleafure of Paris incog ; for I fought Vauclan to claim my debt, but fought him in vain.

Every thing was ready for my depar- ture ; I had taken leave of fome truly worthy and refpectable friends : Scipio was actually placing my luggage on the chaife, when I was ftopped once more by the Rev. Mr. Hilliard, whofe grief and terror had rather difordered his intellect. When he could fpeak to be underftood, it appeared that certain officers of the po- lice had feized his unfortunate pupil at his own lodgings, whither he returned only
that

that morning, and had carried him he knew not whither.

The fecret of all this, my dear Judith, is not to be trufted in a letter. It is fufficient to tell you, he had ftumbled at a mafquerade upon no lefs a man than the Duke d'Artois, whom, in the charaƈter of a highland-feer, he had affronted with true Englifh fpirit and licence. The Duke, on proper reprefentation, was fo good as to pardon the offence, on condition of his leaving Paris. An exprefs from Lady Moreton arrived during his confinement, preffing him to return home direƈtly, if he would fee his Father alive. We are only detained by another litter of debts; and very foon I hope to receive confolation for my imprudence in the affeƈtions and fmiles of a fifter.

Say every thing *proper to fay* to my dear uncle and aunt, and prepare them to receive the prodigal,

JAMES LAMOUNDE.

MISS LAMOUNDE,

T O

MISS EDWARDS.

Kirkham, Jan. 9, 1788.

IN my laſt I gave you due notice of the arrival here of Sir Antony Havelley's precurſor. I now announce the arrival of himſelf, muffled for a Siberian winter, and fatigued to death by the jolting of his chaiſe twenty miles upon a Lancaſhire road. He was immediately conducted to his apartment by Monſieur Tuiffele, his valet, who, according to his cuſtom in caſes of extreme fatigue, gave him thirty drops of a cephalic tincture, prepared at Paris; then laid him gently to reſt, and, excluding the ſun's troubleſome rays, left him to repoſe, till it became neceſſary to dreſs for dinner.

Sir

Sir Antony's dreffing-room joins Mifs Thurl's, and we happened to be at our toilette when Mr. Tuiffele entered to raife his mafter from his bed of foft repofe. "Lard! fays Sir Antony — at three! dine at three! What a facrifice to confanguinity am I neceffitated to make!"

This exordium excited our curiofity, and we never thought of the wickednefs of gratifying it by lift'ning.

"Haft thou feen any of the Goths, Tuiffele?"

"*Vai fait une connoiffance wid de Cuiffinier, et wid de boutelier.*"

"And what is the ftate of things in this gloomy manfion?"

"*Monfieur Turl, le feigneur de Paroiffe* keep his apartement wid de gout. *Madame—votre tante—*do keep hers wid de

vat

vat you call—de rheum—*la toux*. *Monfieur l'Heritier gone á la ville—et Mademoiselle s'accommoder*. She be handfome, *comme ange* — Sir Antony — fhe toufh your heart."

" I fuppofe her accomplifhments are all Englifh, and divinely ruftic, Tuiffele."

" She ave de beauté naturelle."

" Prithee what can nature do for a woman of fafhion ? The cofmetic blooms fo infinitely excel the natural. The adornments — what has nature to do here, but give the colours ? But no Englifh woman, Tuiffele, is born to captivate my heart. The fex at Paris furpafs the fex at London with fuch an infinity of fuperiority. The graces, indigenous at Paris, in London are exotics."

" I do allow de fuperiorité, comme Paris had de finifh of de politeffe of Sir Antony Havelley."

2

I suppose the master returned the compliment, but we could not give ourselves the trouble to hear any more.

Before dinner, Sir Antony paid his respects to his uncle and aunt, after which he joined the Rector of the parish, Miss Thurl and I in the dining-room, and paid his respects with such a terrible quantity of grace, that, like Sir Charles Grandison, of ever graceful memory, he seemed quite encumbered with it.

We had no sooner sat down to table, than we were disturbed by the tumultuous entry of the 'squire, in dirty boots, buckskin breeches, and hair dressed by the wind, whilst the baronet was all elegance and taste. " Cousin, Sir Antony, says the 'squire, shaking him by the hand till the blood mounted into his cheeks—you be heartily welcome—I'm as glad to see you as glad—This is Jack Cornbury, cousin, a comical dog; but come, let's mind dinner,

dinner, and then you fhall tell us about foreign parts."

Sir Antony made one or two fmall inflexions, but his elegant magazine of words afforded none proper to anfwer his extraordinary coufin; an air of diffatisfaction was repreffed by a fmile of contempt. — During dinner every one talked a little, except Sir Antony, who had the humour of filence ftrong upon him. Peftered with that favage remains of iflandic barbarity, the drinking of healths, his condition would have been infupportable; but for a large pier-glafs, commodioufly oppofite, which, by its elegant reflexions, infpired him with gratitude to nature and Paris, for the difference between himfelf and thefe animals of the plains.

Grace being faid, Mifs Thurl enquired of Monfieur Tuiffele what wine his mafter drank?

" *Toujores le claret, Madame.*"

" Blood,

" Blood, fays the 'fquire, it will rot your guts out, coufin ; but come—let's have a bumper to Church and King."

" The politer nations, fays Sir Antony, have laid afide the cuftom of drinking toafts.

" Why fo ? — fays the 'fquire — it's hearty, and promotes good fellowfhip."

" There are, Sir, who think it blunts the nice fenfibility of the nerves, and confequently deftroys the finer affections."

" Finer affections ! What be thofe ? By George, I'm never more loving than in my cups."

Sir Antony directed the fmiling difdain to the mirror, which returned the ineffable image ; then wrapping himfelf in confcious importance, feemed determined to all poffible filence.

                                " When

" When men are drunk, ſays Miſs Thurl, there is no predicting with any certainty whether they will hug, or knock one another down."

" If we do quarrel now and then, ſiſter, it's all over when we be ſober; and what's life if we can't be merry?"

" Nothing ſo vulgar, brother, as noiſy merriment. Lord Cheſterfield baniſhed laughing from the beau monde."

" More fool he, ſiſter; and ben't the bo-moon made of fleſh and blood. Now for my part, I can't help laughing when I'm merry enough, if I was ſure to be hanged."

" I dare ſay Sir Antony never laughs."

Sir Antony bowed aſſent.

" Well now, that's odd, ſays the 'ſquire; but ben't you melancholy then, couſin, Sir Antony?"

Sir

Sir Antony did not anſwer.

" Melancholy, brother, has been celebrated as the ſweeteſt of all pleaſures, and felt only by the fineſt minds."

" By George, let them take it that like it ; but come, couſin, Sir Antony — do tell us about foreign parts."

Sir Antony took no notice.

" Dear brother, ſays Miſs Thurl, you are ſtrangely ill-bred to-day."

" For what, ſiſter ? I want to know nothing but what's fair : I don't deſire to ſteal any thing. They ſay turnips came from foreign parts, and I ſhould be glad to know which get beſt crops."

" Turnips, brother ? Fie ! A man of quality travel to ſee turnips ! It is not to ſee what is common, but what is curious, that connoiſſieurs go abroad. Sir Antony,

I

I hear, has enriched my late uncle's collection to the amount of ten thousand
pounds."

" With what, sister ?"

" Paintings of the best masters, brother ; fossils, coins, lavas, petrifactions."

" What such as you took me to see,
when I came to see aunt Granger and you
at London ?"

" Yes."

" Now I'd rather ha' laid out ten thousand pounds in a mortgage. For why ?
That's productive, and these are a dead
weight. Mayhap if they were sold again,
they'd not bring o'er half the money —
and when one has seen 'em, one has seen
'em : But come, cousin, Sir Antony, be
you a smoaker ? Parson wants his pipe,
and if Jack Cornbury don't make you
laugh, tell me I'm no conjurer."

Sir

Sir Antony defired to be left with the ladies, who thinking, if he could be taken from the contemplation of that charming image in the glafs, he might be drawn into converfation, fhifted their feats into the bow window, and began by afking a few queftions, alas! of too little importance.

The baronet, indeed, had fcarce any paffion ftronger than that of being thought an engaging gentleman by the ladies. Mifs Thurl informs me, the value of the graceful addrefs, the foft voice, the eternal fmile, and the embroidered coat ; but the perfon who forms a complex idea of Sir Antony's merit, correfpondent with his own, muft take fcience into it as well as tafte ; muft refpect him as a man of fortune, and reverence him as a man of family.

Familiar treatment and trifling interrogatories, were fure figns that the idea was not made up as it ought to be. The

firft,

firſt, Sir Antony knew how to repreſs by
a cool reſerve, but the other perplexed
him long. Sir Antony had obſerved,
that when a man thinks profoundly, he
is not ſuppoſed to hear: He begun then
to think profoundly, and in a ſhort time
acquired ſo well the habit of deep abſtrac-
tion, as to loſe by it one half at leaſt the
ſenſe of hearing.

After ſeveral queſtions, therefore, aſked
by Miſs Thurl, which produced monoſyl-
labic replies, or none at all, I ventured
to aſk his opinion of the Italian ladies.
Sir Antony took the mien of conſidering
the queſtion profoundly; and, after a
minute's pauſe, anſwered, with great politeneſs, they are viviparous, Madam.

Young ladies are too apt to laugh at
ſerious things. It was contrary to all the
rules of politeneſs, yet it muſt be owned
they did laugh a little. Sir Antony had
the goodneſs not to perceive it. Spa-
lawzani, ladies, continued he, has obſerved ſeveral parturitions.

" He

" He is a man-midwife, I suppose, says Miss Thurl."

" Madam, says the baronet."

" But I am not, says I, inquiring into their births, but their manners."

" The manners of confined animals, Madam, replied Sir Antony, are all forced and unnatural, and beneath a philosopher's attention."

" Are Italian husbands still so jealous then, asked I ?"

" Madam ! replies the baronet."

" I apprehend a small mistake, says Miss Thurl. Did you know Sir Antony, Miss Lamounde was enquiring after the Italian ladies ?"

" I ask ten thousand pardons, Madam; I thought it had been after the *simiæ volantes,*

lantes, an African animal, which has lately been the fubject of inveftigation in Italy; the learned cannot determine whether it is bird or monkey. As to the ladies I adore them, and fhould confider the making them the fubject of philofophical difquifition, almoft as blafphemy."

This brilliant compliment ftruck us dumb, and gave Sir Antony liberty to flide back to his beloved contemplation, in which he had fcarce indulged two minutes before he was interrupted by the young 'fquire, who entered fmoaking his pipe : " Coufin, Sir Antony, fays he, pray tell me now what your coat be made of."

In thirty feconds the baronet anfwered, " Of flefh, blood, bones, and feathers; though what the peculiar conformation may be, which permits it to dive, but not to fly, we are yet to learn."

" The

The 'fquire gaped : " By George, fays he, it's the oddeft coat that ever I heard tell of, and Jack Cornbury and I be both out."

" Coat! fays the baronet — I beg a multitude of pardons; but I was really fo abforbed in the confideration of a bird, called the aptenodytes, lately found in the South-fea, that I miftook the nature of the queftion."

" Why it was nothing in the world, coufin, Sir Antony, but to know whether your coat be come from foreign parts."

" Monfieur Condery, taileur to Monfieur le duc d'Orleans, formed and fafhioned it : I believe it is from the loom of Lyons."

" Then, by George, I've loft my money, that's all, and I thought myfelf as fure as fure; for, fays I, coufin, Sir Antony, is an Englifhman, and do you think he would go to carry his ready-money to the Moonfeers, when there's fo many honeft tradefmen at home that would be glad on't? It's natural to love one's country."

"It is common to talk of it, replies Sir Antony; or rather, we may confider it as a fafhion gone and paft. It is now a genteeler thing to be a citizen of the world, and love mankind."

"What all in a lump! Now that's nonfenfe, coufin, Sir Antony; for how can a man love all the people he never fee'd?"

"Have you feen all the people of England, Mr. Thurl?"

"No—can't fay that; but then they be my countrymen."

"Mr. Thurl, all the difference betwixt us is this; you are fond of a name, and I of excellence, whenever I find it."

"And

" And why can't you find it in England ?"

" Probably, becaufe it is not to be found there."

" Now there, coufin, Sir Antony, you be out ; for I heard a gentleman fay, that he heard Sir Jofeph (what's his name that went over all the world) fay, that England, take it for every thing, was the very beft country upon God Almighty's earth."

" Refpecting liberty and law, Mr. Thurl, many people are of that opinion ; but, upon honour, the Englifh taylors do not make the beft coats."

" But why now, coufin, Sir Antony ; I can't fee why."

The baronet caft a glance upon the 'fquire's coat, and then upon his own. " The difference, I fhould think, fays he, is tolerably confpicuous."

" Yours

" Yours be fineſt to be ſure, replies the
'ſquire; but fineſt ben't always beſt. Mayhap, when you ſee our ſtud, couſin, Sir
Antony, you'll take that to be beſt horſe
'at has got fineſt cloths. I cod you'll be
confoundedly nick'd, that's all."

Sir Antony took ſnuff with a polite
air of contempt; and Miſs Thurl, fearing
a quarrel, deſired her brother to retire,
for ſhe was diſordered by his tobacco.

" Ey, ey, ſiſter, I'll go. I want to
offend nobody, not I."

Miſs Thurl thinks it neceſſary to be
doubly obliging to Sir Antony, to recom-
penſe him for her brother's want of politeneſs : My poor endeavours alſo have
tended the ſame way, ſo that we are now
very intimate and eaſy. Sir Antony,
though a coxcomb, is a coxcomb of parts;
and ſince, when he is perfectly awake, he
is good-humoured and deſirous to pleaſe,
we are willing to forgive him his ſelf-im-
portant

portant conceptions, his confequential filence, his dreams, and his abftractions.

Mifs Thurl devotes fome hours every morning to attendance upon her Father and Mother. Some of thofe I feize, and fhall feize to converfe with my Paulina. Thank you for your laft agreeable letter, which having nothing particular to anfwer, I only acknowledge it. I am forry you think the good old Mr. Edwards declines fo faft.

My dear Paulina adieu,

Your own,

JUDITH LAMOUNDE.

JAMES

———

JAMES WALLACE,

T O

PARACELSUS HOLMAN,

Liverpool, Jan. 18, 1788.

NO, dear Holman; of imbecillity, of folly, I may give you sufficient cause to accuse me; of dishonour, never. I own you have been right in your prophecies. Miss Lamounde's absence has convinced me how much I love her. So soft, so tender, so pleasing, are the sensations she inspires, how can I wish to stifle them? They are inmates of my own bosom; there were they born, there shall they die, unknown to all but my friend: So will I govern, so will I controul them— they shall always remain as inactive as innocent. I tell thee, dear Holman, they never shall be known to the dear object who inspires them. Their whole opera-

tion

tion, with regard to her, fhall be filent refpect, and dutiful attention. Rather than injure her, I would die a thoufand deaths.

Fear nothing for me, my friend, I am mafter of my refolutions. Should Mifs Lamounde ever fufpect me of *more* than a fervant owes, whilft it appears in the form only of fuperior refpect, fhe is too wife to notice it, too good to punifh it. Nay—were it poffible—but it is not poffible—her fenfibility fhould be exacted by it. Should fhe—which is ftill more impoffible—betray a moment of weaknefs— it is mine to be the guardian of her fame and honour, and I will guard them well. Rather than permit her to indulge a fentiment of degradation, I will quit her prefence for ever.

Adieu,

JAMES WALLACE.

E 4   PARACELSUS

———————

PARACELSUS HOLMAN,

T O

JAMES WALLACE.

Allington, Jan. 24, 1788.

DOST thou remember a certain king, James Wallace (king Canute, I believe) who faid to the waves of the fea— "ftop—come no farther, on forfeit of your heads." I am a king; yet the waves rolled on, and would have falted majefty, if majefty had not ran away : In which predicament, I fay, thou ftandeft, and haft juft as much reafon to fuppofe thyfelf able to ftop the waves of paffion, as king Canute had, to be able to ftop thofe of the fea.

Wallace, I forrow for thee. Can a fair face fo blind the judgment of one that *was* a man, that he cannot perceive how

he

he entangleth himself—amongst the possibles and impossibles. Weak reasoner! If thou art still a man—know thyself in man.

When first I did myself the honour to warn thee of this folly, it was light. A single finger, wouldst thou have applied it, would have pushed it from thee. Now it requires thy whole hand. Soon, James Wallace, too soon, all the muscular motion in the power of thy will, will not move it from its seat—for thy will, will have no power. Am I not now another mentor, preaching in vain to a fond Telemachus. Would I could push thee off the rock! — But I have not at present strength and spirits sufficient to quarrel with thee to any considerable amount. My Father is ill; and, though unaltered in sentiment, I find myself altered in feeling. The cause of his illness is ——No —I will never tell thee another of his follies till he gets well, and into his old habit of abusing me.

Farewell,

E 5   PARACELSUS HOLMAN,

―――――――

MISS LAMOUNDE,

TO

MISS EDWARDS.

Prefcot, Jan. 30, 1788.

I HAVE this inftant parted, not without tears, from my dear and amiable
Mifs Thurl, who has brought me fo far
on my road home, and where I am under
the neceffity of waiting a few hours for
horfes, the Earl of D―― having, as
they call it, fwept the town. In what
can I better employ my time than in
writing to my equally dear Paulina?

I had been a fortnight at Kirkham,
without once hearing from Liverpool. I
had wrote to my uncle, and had not been
favoured with an anfwer. I had thought
it poffible that Wallace might have rode
over; for fure it was eafy to conceive that
in

in that time I might have some orders to execute. In short, my dear Paulina, I was peevish at being so neglected, and could not help expressing some discontent to my friend; but from this little anxiety I was yesterday morning relieved by the post, which brought me the following letter from my uncle:

"I wish you would come home, Judith; I *want* you. This is a greater compliment than ever I expected to have paid a woman; for, in general, to depend upon these creatures for happiness, is not of a wise man; but your aunt and I have tried to mend each other so long in vain, that I am weary of the retort courteous, and she will no longer give herself the trouble to scold. Wallace, indeed, took care I should not die of a calm, for he has suffered me to have little rest by day: However, the Dorrington affair is now over; they have agreed to accept two-thirds of the real estate, and finish at once law, poverty, and humility. How

E 6

Mrs.

Mrs. Dorrington is to reward Wallace, I
know not.   Adequately, she cannot; and,
being a woman, ten to one she thinks
more of a new gown: However, he has
too much spirit to trouble her with any
claim, if he lives; and if he dies, which
is of the two the more probable circumstance, she will quit her score at an easy
charge.   What think you this restless and
enterprizing spirit has been about since
you went; no less than a duel with an
Irish sea captain ! The fellow cannot forget that he is, or ought to be a gentleman, and this want of memory makes
him disgrace *his cloth*.   Both the combatants were wounded, but neither mortally ;
yet Wallace is really in danger from an
excess in weakness.   I am sorry; he is a
gallant fellow, but always in mischief.
Come, Judith, and fan away a black va-
pour that hovers round me ; for, though
I am ashamed to confess it, something is
wanting to my happiness when thou art
absent."

Thy **wife** uncle,

PAUL LAMOUNDE.

A faint ficknefs came over me while I read this letter, my Paulina: Mifs Thurl kindly enquired the caufe. " See how affectionately my uncle writes, anfwered I, giving her the letter; I am exceffively concerned to give him the leaft uneafinefs, and muft leave you this very day."

" Really, my dear, fays this arch, teazing creature, you are a pattern for all dutiful nieces that are and are to be. Your confanguineal fenfations are arrived at the ultimate degree of perfection. There are people in this degenerate age, who would find it difficult to believe.—— Are you fure, my dear, your old uncle, though a very good uncle, is the fole efficient caufe of thefe emotions?"

" Sure! Yes — what elfe can?"

" Nay, I know not. It was poffible to fuppofe, that humanity for a fuffering domeftic might have fome fhare."

" I

" I hope I don't want humanity, my dear Mifs Thurl."

" No—my dear Mifs Lamounde — I don't accufe you of it. I even think—humanity may claim its fhare in this little tumult."

" The accent of your *humanity* gives me *your* idea of it ; but, my dear Mifs Thurl, the idea is whimfical and unkind."

Mifs Thurl took me by the hand, and, in a foftened voice, faid, " I have no un-kindnefs at my heart, my dear. If plea-fantry on this fubject be difagreeable to you—I lay it afide."

" You fhall part with it for a moment only, to tell me your meaning ferioufly and plainly."

" You love Mr. Wallace."

I abfolutely ftarted, Paulina. "Good
God! whence can you have derived fuch
a fufpicion?"——She fmiled.

"But no matter whence. The very
idea is terrible!"

"Why, my dear Mifs Lamounde?"

"How can you afk? In love with my
footman!"

"I know of no prohibition iffued by
nature's council."

"The finger of fcorn would be always
pointed at me."

"Yes—arrets againft fuch things are
always iffuing from the court of pride;
and you, like moft females, acknowledge
its authority. I, no more than you,
fhould dare to be happy againft the good
pleafure of the talking ladies; and yet it
is often hard upon a poor woman to be
forced to reft fatisfied with a fhadow."

"If

" If you think I have this weaknefs, my dear Mifs Thurl, fure you would not endeavour to encourage it ?"

" No — dear Mifs Lamounde ; but it is a fubject I fcarce know how to treat ; it is moft truly delicate.   If your happinefs is concerned, how can I plead againft your happinefs ? Or treat, as a mere fervant, a man of more exalted merit, a man of more fenfe, learning, fpirit, and generofity, than youwould, perhaps, find amongft people of fortune, and pleafe you, in ten years, even by the help of a candle."

" Sure I may be charmed with goodnefs, without taking it for a hufband : Befides, were I convinced I had the requifite affection for him, I ought to know alfo that he had the requifite affection for me."

" Oh, yes—if that's a doubt, it ought to be cleared up ; and yet, his unaffuming modefty on one fide, and your delicacy

on

on the other, it may be a fecret to your-
felves, twenty years after it has been
known to all the world befide."

" The world is not fo fagacious as my
friend, though it muft be owned it fees
often enough beyond the truth; fo for
once I hope do you, my dear."

" We fhall fee, as Sally fays."

" I took the proper opportunity to pay
the compliment of leave-taking of the
old 'fquire and his lady; and the important concern of my departure was foon
known throughout the houfe. For the
laft time, this feafon at leaft, Mifs Thurl
and I indulged ourfelves in our favourite
walk to a pleafing grot, furrounded with
fhrubs, and decorated with many beauties,
by the hand of my fair friend.

We were foon after joined by Sir Antony Havelley, who had ventured out in
the cold of July, wind N.N.E. with no
other

other precaution than two muflin handker-
chiefs about his fenfitive neck. He looked a little melancholy, and had a tender
caft with his eyes, which, after the ufual
falutations, he threw alternately upon me
and the fhell-work.

It was fome minutes before filence was
broke; Mifs Thurl and I, both amufing
ourfelves with forming a conjecture whether my beauties, or the beauties of the
grot, would be the firft fubject of the
baronet's elocution. To the mortification
of my vanity, it broke out upon fhell-
work; upon the fhells, and upon the vaft
variety of animals which inhabit them.
This led him to a defcant of the loco-
motive powers, in the midft of which a
doubt appeared to ftrike him, and brought
him back to thoughtfulnefs and filence;
but the account was really curious and
interefting, and we wifhed him to continue it. After a lapfe of three minutes,
and perceiving his eyes once more fixed
upon me, I ventured to requeft a further
explanation of the loco-motive powers.

" Alas!

" Alas! my dear Mifs Lamounde, fays he, after a few feconds—what avails the power of loco-motion, unlefs we could move along with the dear objects which fill the heart with its firft and fupreme delight? You leave Kirkham to-morrow. All is gone when you are gone; for what is left but ignorance and rufticity?"

Mifs Thurl rofe without fpeaking, and made the baronet a curtefy down to the ground. It awaked him. " My dear, Mifs Thurl, fays he, I fhall die with confufion, if you imagine I intended in the leaft to involve you in this cenfure. I proteft, my dear coufin, I cannot breathe, I cannot exift—till I am affured you acquit me of fo barbarous an intention."

Mifs Thurl fmiled.

" Upon the honour of a gentleman, Madam—it had been a folecifm in common fenfe, as well as politenefs, to apply terms to you which are fo totally inapplicable,

plicable. Pardon the indiscretion, my dear Madam. It was solely owing to an unfortunate abstraction, which fixing my ideas upon one object, I overlooked the rest of the universe."

" I pardon you freely, Sir Antony, replied Miss Thurl; but how can I pardon myself for being, upon so tender an occasion, the ill-omened bird of interruption ?"

I felt the rising blush, Paulina, and rebuked my too-gay friend with a look.

" Nay, Miss Lamounde, said she in answer, you cannot deny but that it had all the appearance of a beginning declaration, and in terms so sweet! I am angry at my own indiscretion."

" I own, says the baronet, with the most gallant air imaginable, I own my fair enslaver." Then taking my hand — " You, Madam, said he, are the queen of
my

my affections. I lay at your feet a heart which has withstood the fairest eyes of Italy and France. I crave permission to escort you to Liverpool, and that you will honour my carriage with your conveyance."

"No"—hold there, cousin, Sir Antony, cries the young 'squire, coming from behind the grot—"She be our guest, not yours. As to your making love to her, why that's as she and you can agree: I've nothing to do with it, but I'll see her home safe and sound. She may have as many sweethearts as she likes; and, tho' she tied my hands up while she's at Kirkham, I'm free to court her as well as you when she's out of the parish; and seeing I fell in love with her before you ever see'd her, I don't see why I haven't a bit of chance. Mayhap you may think your title sets you uppermost; but I can tell you she don't matter titles; she told me so herself; didn't you, Miss?"

"Brother,

" Brother, fays Mifs Thurl, one would imagine you had been drinking this morning, or had loft your fenfes."

" Why fo, fifter? If I have had a whet, I don't fee 'at I'm a bit lefs fenfible : Only they told me Mifs Lamounde was to go to-morrow ; fo it vexed me, and I pulled a little deepifh out of a bowl of milk-punch ; and then I run up to the Druid's Cave, and then back again down to the Grot here ; and fo, finding you all together, I'd a mind to hear a bit what was going on ; that's the fhort and the long on't."

" But then you need not be rude to any body, nor lofe fight of good manners."

" No more I don't, fifter ; only you be fo dainty and froppifh."

" I beg, Mifs Thurl, fays Sir Antony, you will not give yourfelf the leaft trouble on my account ; I have feen human

nature

nature in all its forms. I am furprized at nothing—except that my uncle fhould chufe to give his fon and heir the education of a boor."

" By George — coufin, Sir Antony — I've had a better education than yourfelf— I'll lay you a guinea on't, and Jack Cornbury fhall hold ftakes. What I knows is ufeful."

" Really, Mr. Havelley Thurl" anfwered the baronet with great dignity of contempt, " your language and fentiments are fo below the gentleman, I chufe to decline all converfation with you."

" What! becaufe I can't jabber French, and my coat's made by an Englifh taylor, and becaufe I don't know nothing about burning mountains and porcupines; and becaufe I don't lay out my money in ftones and cockle-fhells. No, no—coufin, Sir Antony, as big a fool as I be, I a'nt fool enough for that, neither."

" This

" This is intolerable, brother; you have neither decency nor good manners."

" I fay I have fifter; if any body hits me a flap o'th' face, it's good manners to return it. Did'nt he call me a boor juft now, and as good as fay I was not a gen-tleman ?"

" I doubt it is too true, brother."

" Womens tongues are no flander, fifter. You be always taking part with any body that abufes me; and I cod, if coufin, Sir Antony, had not been half a woman, I fhouldn't ha' taken it fo quietly."

" Ladies — fays Sir Antony — I kifs your hands. *Jufq' au revoir.* Mr. Havelley Thurl, your moft obedient. I fhall find a time to renew the converfation, when you are more *compos mentis.*"

" There now, fays the 'fquire, that's as much as to fay I'm drunk. By George, clenching

clenching his fift—and I fhall find a time to knock thy lantern jaws together." — The baronet was out of hearing.

" Come—Mifs Lamounde—fays my friend, let us go home, and leave this hair-brained wretch to quarrel with the trees."

" Well then—you may go—if you be fo frumpifh. I came out of love and pure good-will, to be forry about Mifs Lamounde's going away to-morrow, and to offer to take her. If you was but a little better humoured, and more like a fifter, I don't fee 'at it would hurt you. As to Mifs Lamounde, I've done nothing whereby fhe could be offended. I've never offered to court her, nor fay a word to her about love; and I take it unkind fhe fhould let coufin, Sir Antony, court her before my face."

The 'fquire ftalked indignantly away.

As

As foon as Sir Antony got back to the hall, he gave orders for his departure in three hours. Thefe he employed in taking leave of his uncle and aunt; and in writing the two following letters, which, without foliciting an interview, he ordered to be delivered the inftant of his departure.

To Mifs Thurl,

Moft amiable Coufin,

A lady of your fupreme accomplifhments, and enlarged underftanding, will not be furprized that, after the rencounter of this morning, I fhould take a fudden leave of Kirkham. I hope, however, the perfon of the charming Mifs Lamounde will be the connecting band of friendfhip and confanguinity between you, and

Your moft obedient fervant,

ANTONY HAVELLEY.

My

My billet was thus addreſſed :

To Miſs Lamounde,

    Madam,

    When a gentleman is ſo unhappily ſituated, that he is hourly expoſed to ignorance and inſult, he need not fear the diſapprobation of a lady of Miſs Lamounde's ſpirit, ſenſe, and taſte, for aſſerting his own dignity, and for leaving a place where, what is due to a gentleman, is ſo little known or regarded. I ſhould have been happy, Madam, to have had the honour of conducting you in ſafety to Liverpool; but, as this is not permitted, I take the liberty to requeſt your permiſſion, at ſome future, more convenient time, to throw myſelf at your feet, in order to demonſtrate how inconteſtibly I am, Madam,

    Your moſt humble and devoted ſervant,

ANTONY HAVELLEY.

So

So you fee, my Paulina, *at fome future, more convenient time,* what a chance I have of being a lady. I give you all the interim to increafe your veneration, and am, not at all the lefs at prefent,

My dear Paulina's friend and fervant,

JUDITH LAMOUNDE.

PARACELSUS HOLMAN,

T O

JAMES WALLACE.

Allington, Feb. 5, 1788.

A REPORT is fpread here that you have fought a duel with an Irifh captain, are wounded, and in danger. At what an inftant has fate oppofed my duty to my friendfhip.

My Father's languor increafing, I put him under the care of doctor C———, our
.beft

beſt phyſician, whoſe preſcriptions were duly adminiſtered; notwithſtanding which, a paraliſis, preceded by manifeſt marks of mental imbecility, came on, and took away one half his muſcular power, and his ſpeech intirely : But for this I would have flown to my friend ; but to leave a Father to die, moſt probably in my abſence — would it not have incurred the reproach of others, and my own remorſe ? Dear Wallace write, or cauſe to be written, one line to eaſe the anxiety of

PARACELSUS HOLMAN,

JAMES WALLACE,

T O

PARACELSUS HOLMAN.

Liverpool, Feb. 9, 1788.

I AM weak, my friend, but not in danger. When I have ſtrength I will inform you of the cauſe. Be ſatisfied ;

F 3 I have

I have not incurred difhonour or difgrace. Perform your duties to your Father, as long as you have a Father. When you have him no more, come and receive, what you muft give, comfort from your friend,

JAMES WALLACE.

———————

MISS LAMOUNDE,

TO

MISS THURL.

Liverpool, Feb. 9, 1788.

I Promifed my dear Mifs Thurl to give her a fair and candid account of what is doing here, without and *within*. I will fulfil this promife to the beft of my power. Deception would, indeed, be folly; for if I am fick—and I fear I am not well—who but you can be my phyfician?

My uncle received me with that grumbling cordiality, that I have been accuf-
tomed

tomed to love in him. My aunt — I
know not how — she seemed to make an
effort to be kind. We had not been long
seated before I asked how Wallace did?
This simple question, my dear Caroline,
was thrice upon my lips before I could
ask it; and, though I strove for compo-
sure, I asked at last with inward commo-
tion. "Poor fellow! says my uncle, he is
amazingly weak; you must pay him a
visit, Judith: He has great gratitude for
small kindnesses. Your aunt has been
good to him; and, I dare say, he has
told her she is the first of her sex in be-
nignity. You, perhaps, will be an angel."

"It would be extraordinary, brother, if
you was to make a speech without a sarcasm
at me. If doing good deserves no better,
I wonder what doing ill might expect. I
suppose I know Christian duties as well
as you, brother; and, I think, kindness
to the sick and afflicted one of the first of
them."

F 4

"The

" The very quinteffence, dear Beck, and I congratulate thee on the difcovery. This, I believe, is thy firft effay."

" I fancy you are miftaken, brother; there is no neceffity for making a boaft. and oftentation of good works."

" No, fure. The more private, the more Chriftian-like; and thine are done in the moft Chriftian-like manner poffible."

My aunt anfwered this only with, you are a provoking creature, brother, and fo the dialogue ended.

I took the firft opportunity to vifit Wallace, who had been accommodated, by the kindnefs of my aunt, with an apartment on the fecond floor, his bed being in an adjoining clofet. He was fitting with his back to the door, his cheek refting upon his hand, and involved in contemplation. I ftepped foftly round, and prefented myfelf before him.

A

A delirium of a moment feized him, and he funk upon the back of his chair. He recovered inftantly. A hectic flufh came over his cheek. He rofe, bowed, and made an effort to fpeak: He was, however, unable to ftand, and, having fat down again, feemed on the point of falling from his chair; I was obliged to fupport him: His head refted on my waift. I could neither leave nor affift him. My falts were unthought of: In fhort I was diftracted. You may judge how little felf-government I was miftrefs of, when I tell you that, by an involuntary motion, upon his pale and dying face, I laid my own, and wet it with my tears. Perhaps, alfo, he was infenfible to his own motions; for his arm had moved, and fome how had placed itfelf around my waift, had preffed it; I even felt the motion of his lips: It was vaftly alarming—and reftored me to a due fenfe of my fituation. I was angry too—or thought I was; and, looking on him with a frown—Good God! fays I—Mr. Wallace! What free-

dom!

dom! What! Do you know to whom —
I ſtopt. I know nothing, anſwered he,
but that I was in Heaven, whence your
anger has recalled me on earth.

" Have I not reaſon to be angry ?"

" Alas! Madam, I know not; for I
meant no offence, nor knew that I com-
mitted any."

" It is not very reſpectful at leaſt, ſo
to indulge ſudden impulſes of fancy."

" As well, Madam, you might accuſe
me of parricide—of any vice—of every
vice—as want of reſpect for you."

" I am a young woman, Mr. Wallace,
and ſenſible of my own imperfections. I
have no claim to greater reſpect than you
would pay to any other perſon in my
ſituation."

" No

" No claim, Madam! but I beg pardon. I know not how far I may even praife without offence."

" I am not forry to be thought well of by you, Mr. Wallace; but I cannot applaud outreè fentiments, even in my own favour."

" I know not, Madam, that I have ever given unlicenfed way to any fentiment that could injure you : Rather than do this, I would be — as I now am — miferable for ever."

There was fomething in the manner of this, my dear Mifs Thurl, fo touching—I cannot exprefs it—I could not immediately anfwer — I could not fupprefs fome tears. At length I faid—" You are very low fpirited, Mr. Wallace — What is it that makes you fpeak in this defponding ftrain ?"

" Your anger."

F 6 " No—

" No—I'm not angry, Mr. Wallace— that is—I excufe—I pardon what is paft— provided — but we'll talk no more of it. We muft endeavour to get you well as foon as poffible. To-morrow, I hope, to find you more chearful."

I retired to my own apartment, my dear Mifs Thurl, and gave way to a copious fhower of tears; they could not intirely relieve me: I became capable, however, of fome very ferious reflection. The cafe now, my dear, I doubt, is too plain on both fides; but it is eafier fure to eradicate the infatuation, than to bear the obloquy and contempt confequent upon its gratification.

The three fubfequent days, not daring an interview, I contented myfelf with fending frequently to inquire after his health, and with taking care that he had every thing proper to recruit his ftrength, in which, indeed, I was moftly fuperfeded by my aunt. On the fourth day, not fatisfied

tisfied with myſelf, I ventured a viſit, and began the interview, with hoping he was better.

" I am better, Madam, replies he, much better; but I am ſorry—and aſhamed—that——."

" That what ? Mr. Wallace.

" It is impoſſible to repay your generous goodneſs but with gratitude."

" But with gratitude ! Well, continued I, ſmiling, I ſhall remain content ; and what pray, ſince you hold gratitude ſo cheap, do you exact from Mrs. Dorrington ? How great ſoever may be my merit in wiſhing you health and happineſs, I cannot think it equals the reinſtating a wretched, undone family in eaſe and affluence."

" I have been your ſervant, Madam, ſays he, with a penſive air, and you never
permitted

permitted me to perceive I was one. — Once for all, Madam, let me return you thanks for all your goodnefs; and be not offended if I fay, upon whatfoever country I may be thrown, in whatever fituation fortune may place me, your happinefs will always be my prayer, always the firft wifh of my heart."

"I thank you," Mr. Wallace, fays I, turning to the window to look upon nothing, and to hide the ftarting tear. How weak I was! my dear Caroline.

"Then you intend to leave us, Mr. Wallace?"—He bowed his anfwer.

"I hope, fays I, you will be benefited by the change; and give me leave to affure you, if my purfe or intereft can be ufed to your fervice, you are welcome to confider them as your own."

"O God!" fays he. I had no other anfwer.

"May

" May I enquire into your intentions and profpects ?"

Half fuffocated — " No, Madam, anfwered he, I beg you will not."

" I know, fays I, my fervice is beneath you ; nor do I wonder you fhould wifh to change it."

" Good Heaven ! Madam, fays he, with no fmall emotion, how much do you miftake ! I never thought your fervice beneath me ; I never wifhed to change it : It has been to me a fource of happinefs unknown before ; but ——."

" But what !" fays I, in a tremulous and foftened accent.

" There is an invincible neceffity, Mifs Lamounde."

" Of what is it compofed ?" afked I, in a fmiling fort of manner,

" It

" Of honour, Madam ; of probity, of every thing that ought to influence man to good." I thought he would have fwooned.

" You feem faint, Mr. Wallace; pray fit down : Smell at thefe falts. I am exceedingly forry to fee you fo weak."

Mr. Wallace did fmell at the falts, Caroline; and alfo, with fuch an air of veneration and refpect, I could not poffibly be angry, did imprint a kifs upon the foft hand that held them.

" I wifh you would think of nothing at prefent, but to get well. You delay your recovery by anxiety. Come—fays I — laying my hand upon his — promife me to wait my brother's coming—he cannot be long."

" It would be the pride of my life to obey you, Madam ; but ——."

" No

" No more buts—I muft be obeyed."

" How fweet would be obedience ——
if ——."

" If obedience were inclination — I
fuppofe: However, lay them all up, thefe
buts and ifs—get well—and we will exa-
mine their validity. Goodmorrow."

I have wrote you this afternoon, my
dear Mifs Thurl, the conference of this
morning, and wait your judgment. To
any man but Wallace I fhould reproach
myfelf for having faid too much. To
him I can fcarce forbear it, for having
faid fo little. Tell me, dear Caroline,
on which fide I have erred.

Your affectionate,

JUDITH LAMOUNDE.

JAMES

JAMES WALLACE,

TO

PARACELSUS HOLMAN.

On Board the *Caithnefs*, *Liverpool*,
February 15, 1788.

THAT which I fuppofed impoffible,
dear Holman, is come to pafs. In
a delirium I have difcovered my love;
it did excite her fenfibility. In a fubfequent conference fhe betrayed the moment
of weaknefs. I *will be* the guardian of
her fame and honour : I *will* quit her
prefence for ever, though my death may
be the confequence. The ftate of my
fpirits will not permit me now to acquaint
you what events have caufed my prefent
fituation ; but I will write them fully
when I get to fea. I fhould be happy
to embrace you before my voyage; but
we fail in three days, and I charge you

not

not to leave your Father. The firſt veſſel we meet homeward-bound ſhall bring you a large packet.

Dear Friend, adieu,

JAMES WALLACE.

MISS THURL,

T O

MISS LAMOUNDE.

Kirkham, Feb. 18, 1788.

IT is impoſſible, my dear Judith, to be a perfect judge of the queſtion of which you deſired my deciſion, for want of the principal evidence As far as words went, I decide that you have no cauſe to reproach yourſelf: They ſeem to be words of mere humanity; yet, to a man in love, they might ſeem words of kindneſs. But how went looks and tones, my dear? In this caſe I ſhould have re-
lied

Tied more on them than upon words. It feems, however, as if your fate, relative to Mr. Wallace, was drawing to a crifis : I beg you will not delay the communication.

The letters wrote to you and me, my dear Mifs Lamounde, were not the fole products of the elegant pen of Sir Antony Havelley ; my brother had the fame honour. I have taken great pains to get at the bottom and top of the whole tranfaction, words, thoughts, and deeds ; and, by Mr. Cornbury's affiftance, I have fucceeded. Read — read — young woman, and lament the ravages your fatal beauties caufe.

C O P Y.

Mr. Havelley Thurl,

" As you affert your title to the rank of gentleman, I fuppofe you know the ufage on the receipt of grofs affronts. I expect you will meet me in the field with piftols or the fmall fword, as may pleafe you

you beſt. Since inconvenience often en-
ſues by the laws of this country to the
ſurvivor, if one gentleman happens to
fall, it will beſt be prevented by ending
the conteſt abroad, upon the confines of
France and Flanders: I therefore appoint
Bethunè, a town of France, for the place
of our meeting on the firſt day of March
next, there to determine the other necef-
ſary points; and ſhall come attended only
by one gentleman, my ſecond, and my
ſurgeon."

ANTONY HAVELLEY.

Immediately after the fracas of the
morning, my brother had gone to his
friend Jack Cornbury's, with a ſturdy reſolution, ſeeing Miſs Lamounde was ſo
ungrateful, not to care a fig for her; he
had alſo reſolved not to come to the Hall
whilſt Sir Antony ſtayed. It happened
that Mr. Cornbury's houſe lay in Sir
Antony's road; and my brother had the
pleaſure of ſeeing the baronet and his
equipage paſs by at full ſpeed. The pair
of

of friends had dined, and had advanced into the regions of fun and noife, a bottle a piece deep. This accident produced two bottles more, to drink Sir Antony's good journey; after which my brother, accompanied by his friend, took the road home. His fervant prefented the baronet's letter. My brother read and fwore, and fwore and read, and ftampt with a wonderful degree of wildnefs, to the utter amazement of his friend; and, as he found himfelf endued with an extraordinary quantity of valour, he ftormed, bluftered, and was coming to make you and I partake of the entertainment; but Mr. Cornbury informed him, that it was reckoned cowardly to truft an affair of honour to women; and that men of courage always maintained an inviolable fecrecy, except to that one friend who was to be the fecond: However, it is proper to write Sir Antony an anfwer, to inform him if he accepted the challenge.

My

My brother refented the if, and afked his friend if he looked like a coward? To which Mr. Cornbury anfwered, he knew his courage in the field; but, as he was not much ufed to piftols, and had never learned to fence, he did not know how it would be: However, adds this learned counfellor, the gentleman that's challenged always chufes his weapons.

Before they had gone much farther in confultation, two gentlemen farmers came in to complain of certain infraction of the game laws, which my brother confiders as the magna-charta of country gentle-men. His anger was now turned into a more important channel; they fet in to found folid drinking, and the evening ended with great feftivity.

In the morning my brother was low and nervous. The challenge was the firft thing that entered his head. It muft be an-fwered, and what fignifies put offs; fo taking a few pulls at a bowl of milk-
punch,

punch, his favourite morning's draught, he gathered together as much steadiness of head and hand, as produced the following morceau.

Cousin, Sir Antony,

" I received your epistle, telling me you want to fight me, to the which I am both ready and willing; only I see no occasion to go amongst papishes in foreign parts, when we can do it every bit as well in the county of Lancaster. As to being afraid of the law—it's nonsense. If one man goes to kill another without his consent, that's murder; but if two people be minded to kill one another — why it's their own act and deed—and the law has nothing to do with it; so you see if a man be tried for't, he's always quit.

Now, cousin, Sir Antony, I being the person challenged, you knows have a right to chuse my weapons. Now I don't matter pistols, because a body can't hit a

barn-

barn-door with them twenty yards off—
and for the small sword, Troll, my hound,
knows as much on't — because I never
was a soldier do you see—for I don't like
soldiers—and Father could never get me
to go into militia—for let them fight as
have nothing else to trust to—say I.

So, cousin, Sir Antony, I don't see
why you and I mayn't take a turn or two
at boxing, or else at cudgels, or, mayhap,
you may like quarter-staff; and when it's
o'er — drink a bottle together, and be
friends; for why should a body bear malice? But if you be so bloody-minded,
nothing but death will serve; then I desire we may have fowling-pieces—but not
rifle-barreled—and only a yard and four
inches from mouth to touch-hole. Jack
Cornbury shall stand between us with a
handkerchief, and drop it for signal to
fire, and if I don't fetch you down, say
I'm no shot : So if you like any of these
proposals, name place any where in Lan-
cashire, Westmoreland, or Cumberland;

and I'd rather have any other day in the
year than the 1st of September—for why?
all my best coveys would be shot before
I got back again : However, to shew you
I an't of a blood-thirsty humour, I'd rather gi you only a broken head, or a black
eye—and so make an end on't.

Your loving Cousin,

HAVELLEY THURL.

What think you, my dear, of my brother's answer? If I had not known the
simplicity of his character, I should have
taken it for a ridicule of duelling, but it
is all very honestly meant : Nor does my
brother in the least want courage—but it
is not courage à la mode. What will be
the event of this letter, I know not ; but,
I think, Sir Antony will despise it, and
drop all further notice. I shall watch, in
order to prevent mischief. Pray write
soon to your

CAROLINE THURL.

Is

Is your brother returned? I am half in
love with him for thofe letters from Paris.

PARACELSUS HOLMAN,

TO

JAMES WALLACE.

Allington, Feb. 30, 1788.

I COULD fwear the moon down, Wallace, at thy folly; or I could cry at it,
were it not for difgracing my *toga virilis.*
Juft at a time when I had projected making your country a comfort to you, you
leave it; but if you have not entered into
an engagement, revoke your intention,
and come to me. Thirty miles from Mifs
Lamounde may be as efficacious as three
thoufand. If you will commit yourfelf
to the mercy of the faithlefs fea, almoft
as little to be trufted as a woman, accept
thefe memorials, which I have ordered to
be delivered into your hands: A chafed

G 2   gold

gold watch—a family antique—and two portraits. I have a ftrong fufpicion they were your Mother's; why I think fo I will reveal to no man whilft my Father lives—and then to no man but yourfelf. If I am right in my conjecture, accept them from me as a reftitution; if wrong, as a prefent. I add a memorial of a lefs valuable matter, which I do not afk you to keep for my fake: I hope I live in your heart. Adieu. Though enraged, I wifh you a fafe voyage and fwift return.

Yours,

PARACELSUS HOLMAN.

My Father's life I do not expect many hours.

JAMES

JAMES WALLACE,

T O

PARACELSUS HOLMAN.

The Caithness, March 4, 1788.

YOUR friendſhip, dear Holman, is the healing balm that cures half the evils of my life. At this buſy inſtant I have not time to indulge either in the feeling, or in the expreſſion of it; we are getting under ſail: Ceaſe your anxiety; I ſhall ſoon return. For the memorials of my Mother, if they are of my Mother, I am deeply indebted to you. Can the portraits, think you, be hers and my Father's? From the little I know of my own face, it ſeems to reſemble the gentleman's, and, or I am fond of imagining ſo, in the lady's, is a likeneſs of Miſs Lamounde. I return your fleeting memorial: I do not want it; and you ſay rightly—I have got you in my heart.

JAMES WALLACE.

———————

MISS LAMOUNDE,

T O

MISS THURL.

Liverpool, March 8, 1788.

SINCE I wrote laſt, my amiable friend, I have been much diſtreſſed ; the bitterneſs of it over. I am *now* only perplexed. Effects have happened that ſeem to me greater than their cauſes. I will relate all I know, and hope to be indebted to your clearer comprehenſion for the elucidation of what, at preſent, appears obſcure.

I called in upon Wallace the morning after I wrote my laſt, and found my aunt in his apartment, whom I had not happened to meet there before, though I knew ſhe was ſo kind as to make perſonal enquiries ſometimes. She was ſaying
ſomething

fomething when I opened the door, but
ftopped. I thought fhe looked angry: I
thought alfo that Wallace had a glow
upon his cheek. She bid him good-morrow, and faying, with a fort of tofs of the
head, fhe left him with more agreeable
company, went away. What could all
this mean?

" Is my aunt angry, Mr. Wallace."

" No, Madam, I hope not; I have
given her no caufe."—I then renewed the
difcourfe of the day preceding, concerning his ftay till my brother's arrival. He
looked dejeƈted, and did not anfwer. I
began to intreat; and, I know not how,
had put my hand within the reach of his,
when he, very refpeƈtfully, and to thank
me, I believe, put it to his lips. At this
inftant Sally, my moiety of maid, opened
the door, and, feeing me, was ftepping
back. I ordered her to come in, faying
I was going away; then defiring Wallace
to remember my advice, I withdrew.

G 4

At

At dinner there was a gloom for which I could not account. My uncle was thoughtful, my aunt filent and referved. She retired as foon as the cloth was drawn. I then ventured to afk my uncle if any thing had difcompofed him?

" Yes, anfwered he—woman." After a paufe — " Have you heard any thing about your aunt?"

" No, Sir. Of what nature?"

" Of the nature of woman. She is going to be fool enough to throw away all that blaze of charms fhe poffeffes upon Wallace, if the fellow will be fool enough to take her." Dear Mifs Thurl, how I trembled!

" Is it poffible, Sir, faid I, you fhould believe fuch a thing?"

" Yes—why fhould I not?"

" Dear

" Dear uncle—it is fo improbable.

" That an elderly maiden fhould like a handfome young fellow !"

" Sir, fhe is twice his age !"

" Yes—that adds to the improbability."

" I don't know, dear uncle, but I cannot believe it ; it is fo unnatural !"

" Unnatural ! Judith, you are quite philofophical to-day."

" I mean, Sir, it is fo unlikely."

" Yes—as unlikely as unnatural."—— My uncle then told me his reafons : I will not trouble you with them. If my aunt has follies, *I* ought not to expofe them. My uncle did not convince, but he ftaggered me.

That night he fupped abroad. My aunt kept her apartment; I retired early to
mine.

mine. I wanted to think, my dear Caroline : I never was lefs capable.

In the courfe of our converfation my
uncle had afked me why I was fo agitated?
What was it to me ?

To be fure, my dear Mifs Thurl, it
is nothing more to me than the concern
one naturally takes in having one's relations act wifely. She is her own miftrefs,
and Wallace his own mafter; but there
is fomething vaftly cdd in it. Are mens
minds fo light? It is true he had never
uttered a fyllable; I could never have
forgiven him if he had; but when he was
weak and unguarded—did not his behaviour feem to denote that he had unfortunately imbibed a paffion for——quite
another object? Such thoughts as thefe
diftracted me all night. The following
day—What a day ! I never faw my uncle;
nor did my aunt come down. I paid my
duty to her in her own room, and was re-
warded by filence, and chilling referve.

Moft

Moſt of my hours I ſpent in tears: I only ſent in to Wallace, whom I had not ſpirits to ſee.

The next morning my uncle and I breakfaſted together. He was penſive, and ſeemed unhappy. After our uncomfortable meal was over, I ventured tremulouſly to aſk if he was not well? He anſwered, frowningly — " Not ſick—unleſs in mind."

" Any thing more, Sir, of my aunt?"

" No — anſwered he, ſternly — ſomething of her niece." Then, looking me full in the face — " That dog, Wallace, ſays he, has the power of faſcination, and every female in the family, I believe, is deſtined to feel it."

The blow, my dear Caroline, was ſudden: I felt the colour mount into my cheek. I could not ſpeak. My uncle cried Humph! catched up his hat and

cane,

cane, and walked out. He did not return till midnight. I had the whole day to myfelf, and I fpent it in tears and in reflection.

At Wallace I was ferioufly angry; for to what could I attribute my uncle's farcafm, but to fome indifcretion of his? Was it then poffible he could have made me the fubject of his difcourfe in fuch a way? Oh! my dear Mifs Thurl, how I was! But is there, as my uncle afks, is there ftability in woman?

The morning opened with a different fcene. William, the coachman, when I was entering the breakfaft-parlour, put in my hands a letter. Read it.

C O P Y.

Madam,

" The crime my heart has dared, I fly to expiate. To quit my country is nothing; for few—very few, indeed, are the

ties

ties that bind me to it: But you — Miss
Lamounde — permit me—now that I am
never to fee you more—permit me, for
the firft and laft time, to fay I love you,
and muft love you, whilft Heaven grants
me memory and reflection. I afk no pardon for prefumption: I have no prefumption—no hope—no profpect—but of defpair. You—Madam—you—I muft fee
no more! At this thought a mift gathers
round me—my fight is obftructed—my
heart fickens. If it were death, how willingly would I embrace it! But I muft
live—to fuffer--perhaps, for the fins of
my parents. May the firft happinefs be
ever yours; and never may a more un-
pleafing fenfation arife in your mind,
than pity for the loft,"

JAMES WALLACE.

It was fortunate my uncle did not rife
this morning fo early as ufual, fo that I
had half an hour to read—and feel. At
length I muftered fpirits to go down,
and

and found my uncle attentive to the perufal of a letter. He faluted me with more placidity than the day before; then looked directly at me, as if he would have enquired of my eyes what paffed in my heart. I had in my eyes, no doubt, traces of the recent tear, which might poffibly difpofe my uncle to fomething like pity.

"You look poorly this morning, Judith."

"I have not flept well, Sir."

"Want of fleep, Judith, is a fymptom of fome difeafe, corporeal or mental; you fhould have advice."

"I don't perceive the neceffity, Sir."

"The very want of perception is often fymptomatic: As for example — when young ladies are in love—a grievous diforder—they can feldom perceive that any thing elfe ails them."

"Shall

" Shall I pour out the tea, Sir ?"

" Where is your aunt ?"

" She has fent word fhe does not come down to breakfaft ; fhe has not flept well, and has a cruel head-ach."

" Humph! It muft have been an odd night, that no woman could fleep in it."

" Would you chufe the hot roles, Sir, or —— ?"

" Judith."——" Sir."

" Are there amongft women any fuch things as candour—ingenuoufnefs—veracity ?"

" Why fhould you doubt it, Sir ?"

" I do not afk after thefe as occafional qualities. When it is a woman's intereft fhe can be good, almoft as eafily as otherwife ;

wife; wife, almoft as eafily as filly: But knoweft thou a woman wherein thefe are permanent qualities? Who can adhere to them upon all occafions?"

"There may be caufes, Sir, wherein the exercife of thefe virtues would be productive of more ill than a temporary fufpenfion of them."

"Love, Judith, produces thefe caufes abundantly."

"I am not acquainted with its effects, Sir."

"Not all its effects, Judith; fome, perhaps."

"Have I fweetened the tea to your liking, Sir?"

"The tea taftes as it ought to do. Nature has fucceeded in all her works, but woman: She could never mean to create fo verfatile an animal."

"My

" My dear uncle, how fhould you comprehend the nature of an animal you have
avoided all your life ?"

" As I comprehend other natures, by
their effects."

" I am certain I don't at all comprehend the nature of your catechifm this
morning."

" Its origin is here," giving me a letter; it was from Wallace. I opened it,
and tried to read; but, whilft my uncle
obferved me with fuch penetrating keen-
nefs — to underftand was impoffible. I
faw enough, however, to perceive it was
worthy of the writer. My fituation was
diftreffing. I would have given the world
to have retired, and to have indulged in
the luxury of tears : A few fell, notwithftanding my utmoft endeavours for firm-
nefs and compofure. I obtained enough
of thefe to draw Wallace's letter from
my pocket ; and, putting it in my uncle's
hand,

hand, ſaid, " I would do my endeavour that, in one woman at leaſt, my dear uncle ſhould find candour, ingenuouſneſs, and veracity."

My uncle read and read again : I ſuſpect too he was moved with a womaniſh weakneſs, from the pains he took to hide it. At length came the comment. " Why here now, ſays he, this is what you call love and honour ; the very ſtuff that faſcinates young ladies : And you really believe, Judith, that this young fellow is running away, purely to ſtop the tatling of goſſips ?"

" Whatſoever I believe, Sir, is of no importance. Since I am to ſee him no more, no bad conſequences can follow credulity."

" Folly may, my pretty niece ; the folly of thought."

" I hope I ſhall be able to correct it, Sir ; at leaſt conceal it."

" I

" I hope fo too. I am forry, after all, things have taken this turn. To tell thee a fecret, I never yet did fee a young fellow I liked fo well. I had defigns in his favour ; but I did not intend him for a nephew—nor did I much wifh him for a brother-in-law. Betwixt thee and I, Judith, is it thyfelf, or thy aunt, that is the true caufe of this elopement ? Does he run away from a young woman, or an old one ?"

" I am totally ignorant, Sir, of any kind of correfpondence betwixt my aunt and Mr. Wallace."

" And if thou hadft known it, Judith, at which wouldft thou have been moft angry—at him or her ?"

" I had no right to be angry at either."

" Then thou wouldft have been wrong, take my word for it."

" I

"I hope your apprehensions are so, Sir. I own my compassion for an unfortunate young man: I think he has great merit, nice honour, and too strong sensibility; but as to love — dear uncle — I protest ——."

"Reserve the protestation, dear Judith, till thou hast well considered it. I have an appointment this morning: I own too I am not the proper confidante of a young lady — in love or out; but I love thee, though I seldom tell thee of it, and I would have thee happy. All I wish is, you would confide in your brother."

"I promise you I will, Sir."

My uncle gave me a very kind kiss, and went out, leaving me with more tranquil spirits than I had enjoyed many days: Still I had my aunt to encounter, of whom, indeed, I did not stand much in awe; since, if whispers are to be admitted as proofs of folly in me, the same proofs

proofs at leaft lie againft her. Shall I
confefs alfo, my dear Mifs Thurl, I did
not feel myfelf, with refpect to my aunt,
difpofed to pay that deference to her authority and opinions, as to thofe of my
uncle ; fo, half a rebel, I entered her
apartment.

I found her walking up and down, with
hafty ftrides, half dreft, her hair loofe, her
face inflamed. She anfwered my falutations peevifhly, and plainly intimated fhe
did not at prefent wifh for my company.
I retired, with a refolution fhe fhould
defire it before fhe had it again. I am
forry for it, Caroline, but fuch is woman.

Alas! my aunt was more an object of
pity than of anger. She *did* defire my
company the next morning, and fhe received me with tears. They difarmed
me, and I attempted to confole her —
aukwardly, indeed, enough, becaufe the
caufe of her grief was too delicate to be
touched. At length fhe fpoke nearly as
follows,

follows, In which I found more good sense, and more candour, than I had been accustomed to think my aunt possessed; and, instead of lessening, she rather increased my esteem.

" It is possible, my dear Judith, you may attribute these tears and this grief to a wrong cause — to a loss of the hopes, with which I had flattered myself respecting Mr. Wallace: No, my dear, they arise from the shame of having ever entertained any."

" I struggled long against my weakness; but the object of it, with all his merit, was too often before me. I need not expatiate upon this merit, my dear, because you have always acknowledged it, and, if report is right, have felt it."

She said this with a smile. I was going to answer, when she laid her hand upon mine, and said—" I have lost all right of animadverting upon the lesser weaknesses

of

of others. My prefent concern is to acknowledge and expiate my own."

" When I had got over the obftacles
which my pride laid in the way, fuch as
his being a footman, a beggar, the child
of nobody, and others of the like kind, I
determined upon being happy my own
way ; but the difficulty lay in the firft
fteps to be taken to inform the young man
of his good fortune—for fo I had no doubt
he would efteem it.

" There was only one way confiftent
with female decorum. To fpeak in kinder
accents — to become more familiar — and
feem to confider him as a perfon intitled
to efteem. All thefe produced nothing
like what they were intended to pro-
duce. He kept ftill at a moft provoking,
refpectful diftance, and treated me with a
double portion of efteem and regard.

" I now fee clearly how this ought to
have been interpreted ; but then I could
fee

fee nothing but myfelf.   One day I went
fo far as to tell him, I was fure he muft
be a gentleman by birth, and that I fhould
value myfelf upon being able to raife him
to that diftinction, which nature had defigned, and fortune denied.

" But this was not plain enough.   He
had infinite gratitude, indeed—but a word
of warmer import he would never fuffer
to efcape him.

" It would be fruitlefs and tedious to
dwell upon this fubject.   I could not
avoid opening my eyes at laft to the true
meaning of this behaviour—nor refenting
it.   From hints too, which Sally had the
impertinence to let fall, and I the folly
to pick up, I became jealous of you, my
dear; and was actually quarrelling with
him on this fubject when you entered his
apartment a few mornings fince.

" The only inftance of difrefpect he
ever fhewed me was upon my mentioning
your

your name on this occasion. Madam,
says he, to insult Miss Lamounde, is
not to know her; and to possess such a
treasure in a niece, and not to know its
value, I can scarce conceive a greater
misfortune."

" I left him, confirmed in my suspicion
that there was a correspondence betwixt
you, and that to this circumstance I owed
his rejection of me. Hence arose the
manner in which I have behaved lately
to you, and which, I hope, my dear, you
will not remember."

I answered I certainly should not ; and
she must now give me leave to clear myself of the suspicion she had entertained.

This letter, says she, has convinced me
there has been nothing improper on your
part.

Madam,

" For the honour you have done me,
accept my most unfeigned thanks, and do

not

not attribute to any difrefpectful fentiment of you, that I beg leave to decline
it. I am not worthy. Rumours have
arifen, and you, I fear, have imbibed them,
that I have dared to regard my young
lady with other eyes than thofe of duty.
Yes, Madam — I own it—I do love — I
adore her; but, till this inftant, it has
been a fecret and facred fentiment within
my own bofom. I acknowledge her infinite goodnefs, as I do yours, Madam,
during my illnefs; but it is to that goodnefs fhe owes the malignity which now
affails her. I go to defeat it. I go, Madam, to fome other country, that this
may no longer make me the inftrument
of its malice. Wherever I go, I fhall
retain a grateful remembrance for all your
kindnefs"—and am, Madam,

Your moft obedient fervant,

JAMES WALLACE."

I con-

I confided my aunt's *amende honorable* to my uncle, requefting it might never be remembered againft her. " In particular, dear Sir, fays I, have the goodnefs never to make this lapfe, fo well recovered, the fubject of a bon mot."

" Well, well, fays he, if the good ladies of Liverpool will let her flide quietly back into the awful clafs of virgins cenforial, I will not difturb her."

Tranquillity being thus reftored to our houfe, I had time to think of myfelf — and Wallace. I fat down with the utmoft ferenity to my work, and pricked my fingers with great fatisfaction till the fenfation became too lively. I fat down to my piano-forte—tried Abel, Bach, Schobert, Haidn. I was unfortunate in my felection ; every piece was flat. At length I fat down to mufe—and, without thinking of it, I took Wallace's letter from my pocket-book, and read it, more, I doubt, like a woman than like a philofopher. I

tried,

tried, indeed, to be angry, but my pride had not vigour enough for the fupport of turbulent emotions, and I funk into compaffion.

Wallace, my dear Mifs Thurl, is on board a veffel, bound, I fuppofe, to America. He had the good fortune to do a fervice to the captain, a grateful Scotfman, I believe, for he vifited him feveral times during his illnefs: But the poor youth has no money, and what will be his condition abroad without it? Something he has a right to demand for wages; and if humanity were filent, common honefty required that this fomething fhould be paid. I could wifh to fee him, but durft not; there are many reafons to the contrary. I faw none againft my writing, at leaft none I was difpofed to regard. Six efforts, Caroline, I made, to fay exactly what was right and proper. There was fomething too much or too little in all of them. Out of pure wearinefs I was

obliged

obliged to reſt contented with the ſeventh.
Here it is.

Mr. Wallace,

S I R,

" That the reſolution you have taken
to quit this country is prompted by honor
and delicacy I cannot doubt ; nor can I
be entirely at eaſe without making the
acknowledgment. I am ſorry, indeed,
you have conceived ſentiments that ―― ;
but though this is a ſubject on which I
cannot ſpeak, I know not what ſenſe of
propriety ſhould prevent my giving you
ſome teſtimony of my eſteem.

" Why you ſhould chuſe to leave England, rather than ſeek in it an *occupation
worthy of you*, I ſee no cauſe. You yourſelf have taught me, that the beſt uſe of
fortune is to aſſiſt the worthy ; and to
have practiſed the precept upon its author would have been a real ſource of
pleaſure.

H 3

" I

" I afk as a favour your acceptance of the inclofed. Let not your pride be the opponent of your principles : If you refufe it, it will be a proof to me that you no longer defign me a place in your memory. This will be delivered you by a fafe hand, captain Iflay himfelf, who dines here to-day. I excufe your writing back, becaufe, as the captain informs us, he fails to-morrow. I wifh you a good voyage, and fhall always be glad to hear of your health and happinefs.

Your humble fervant,

J. LAMOUNDE."

This letter I fhewed both to my uncle and aunt, who did me the honour to approve it. Will it—and will my general behaviour meet with the approbation of my Caroline ? If not—I fhall again lofe part of the peace of mind I have recovered. Adieu.

Yours,

JUDITH LAMOUNDE.

" My brother is hourly expected."

MISS THURL,

T O

MISS LAMOUNDE.

Kirkham, March. 12, 1788.

AND fo, my dear, your affair turns out one of the moſt common affairs of life—if my clear comprehenſion comprehends the whole of it.

Mr. Wallace is ill. Mrs. Rebecca Lamoúnde, an aged lady, takes care to give him ſweet-meats. The ſervants talk—for why ? as my brother ſays, when they were ill ſhe left them to live or die, as pleaſed God and the apothecary. Judith Lamounde too, a young lady, gives a few ſugar-plumbs; and, though it is a clear caſe, that ſhe gave them from pure humanity, every one does not perceive when humanity is pure. Sally, I dare ſay,

is

is dimfighted as to fuch objects, though there are fome fhe can fee very well; and when fhe fees what fhe does not like, I fuppofe fhe has the talent of painting it in fuitable colours. That kifs of the hand, probably, Sally painted in black, and fhewed it every body, and then you know it is foon a fecret to nobody. Thus things come about, Mifs Lamounde, and, as the world goes, you ought to be much obliged to it, if it takes the trouble to talk about you two or three days on fo flight an oc-cafion.

Nothing here to be talked about. No news of Sir Antony: My brother fays he is not half a man, for not accepting the terms of his challenge. I believe I have ftifled the affair by a letter I wrote to *coufin, Sir Antony*. Havelley defires his fervice to you — not his love — becaufe — though you be a pretty girl — and that's the truth on't—yet pride fpoils beauty.

I defire to hear all that has paffed fince your brother's arrival: In confide-

ration

ration of which, and for other good and sufficient caufes, I do confirm that your conduct has been perfectly proper, and sweetly amiable, let the ladies of Liverpool say what they please, and do testify this by my sign manual.

CAROLINE THURL,

MISS LAMOUNDE,

TO

MISS THURL.

Liverpool, March 16, 1788.

I ACCEPT the sign manual of your approbation, which is, indeed, very neceffary to the obtaining my own; and I will thank you for it, by obeying your commands.

My brother arrived late in the evening, when we had all feparated to our apartments. I was only half undreffed, indeed,

H 5

fo

fo flew down ftairs to bid him welcome; but, finding him extremely fatigued, and more in need of reft than refrefhment, I conducted him to his chamber, and left him to his repofe.

His fervant Scipio, a perfon of fome confequence amongft us, and whom I muft introduce to your acquaintance, by a relation of thofe circumftances which introduced him to ours : Scipio's defires were more alive than his mafter's. As the maids and the coachman were ftill up, Scipio chofe a regale ; and, to heighten the pleafure of it, they gave him the ftate of our houfhold affairs, drawn up after the manner of men, with fome enlargement, I believe, but not on the fide of charity.

However, as they all talked at once, after the manner of women, Scipio arofe in the morning with a mafs of unformed matter in his head, and went to attend his mafter, juft at the inftant my brother

was

was wondering why he had not feen Wallace the evening before. The firft queftion he put to Scipio was—if he had feen him?

No, Scipio anfwered; he have run away.

" Run away!"

" So dey tell a me, Sir."

" Gone away, you mean; left his place."

" Yes, Sir, gone away, run away, both; what de difference?"

" Difference! What—has he run away with more than himfelf?"

" Yes, Sir."

" The devil! What has he robbed the houfe?"

" Yes, Sir."

H 6　　　　　　　" Then

" Then I give up phyfiognomy and Monfieur Lavater for ever. What has he ftole?"

" Two hearts."

" What humour are you in this morn-ing? If thou haft any meaning, Scipio, prithee explain it."

" Me not ver well underftand—but dey do tell a me—dat he have ftole de heart of Madame Lamounde—and de heart of Mifs Lamounde—and run away wid dem beyond fea."

My brother fwore, I believe, a few French oaths, made Scipio give him the little information he was able, and then, with a head as clear as that of Scipio himfelf, he came down to the breakfaft-parlour.

My uncle was there alone, and the fa-lutations were perfectly cordial: After
which —

which—I have heard, fays my brother, a very odd account of the man I fent from Abbeville; it has furprifed me very much. I could not have thought fo young, fo ingenuous as he appeared to be, he could have harboured a corrupted mind.

Why, replies my uncle, gravely, he certainly has been guilty of fome extraordinary things. I take as much care of my money as moft men; but I have not had vigilance enough to keep his hand out of my purfe: Even your aunt Beck has been a fufferer, careful as fhe is; and, to my certain knowledge, he is gone off with a fifty pound bank note that was your fifter's: Indeed, he had very fecret and uncommon ways of fpending money.

And of getting it too, I think, fays my brother.

If, fays my uncle, with continued gravity, he had made his attack upon our

purfes

purfes only, I think, I fhould have forgiven him — but to fteal our hearts! To
thaw the icicles that furround, or fhould
furround, a virgin's heart! To warm the
breaft of frozen age!

Dear Sir, fays my brother, your jefting
upon a fubject of fuch confequence makes
me hope I have been too eafily alarmed;
but in proportion as you filence my fear
you excite my curiofity.

" And here comes Judith to gratify it,
fays my uncle; fhe will give you the
naked truth, as all young ladies do, when
the queftion is love."

" As far as I know the truth, dear uncle, my brother may be affured of knowing
it alfo. I will have no fecrets for him,
no more than I will have for you, Sir,
whenever you pleafe to condefcend to become my confident."

" I

" I am too old, Judith. I should be mingling the laws of prudence with the laws of nature, and, I am told, they seldom mix kindly."

My aunt entered, and changed the conversation. After breakfast, when my uncle had withdrawn to the accompting-house, and my aunt to her domestic matters, my brother took my hand very affectionately, and said, I am referred to you, dear Judith, for information concerning some odd particulars relative to Wallace, but don't be afraid; in a country where Cytherea reigns, it is not likely I should have learned to become a severe censor of slight deviations.

A pretty exordium, brother, answered I : It supposes I have something to confess which requires indulgence.

I own, my sister, I understand it so; it has been told me that Wallace has presumed ———.

" To

" To do what, brother ?"

" To raife his hopes as high as your-felf."

" I believe it is not true, brother."

" What then am I to underftand by my uncle's inuendo about ftealing hearts ?"

" My uncle does my aunt and I the honour to fuppofe we fell in love with Mr. Wallace."

" What ! without foundation ?"

" Oh, no ! One of us did prefume to raife her hopes as high as Mr. Wallace ; but not me, brother—it was my aunt. I will inform you of the particulars more at leifure : But as my aunt has fince been extremely ingenuous, has owned the foi-ble, and repented of it, I beg it may never be remembered againft her."

" Be

" Be it fo ; but it is not for my aunt I am now anxious. Speak, dear Judith, of my fifter."

" Here I ftand, brother, a fimple girl, expofed to all the horrors of catechifm."

" Does Wallace love you ?"

" I think he does."

" Has he declared it ?"

" Yes."

" Have you encouraged, or rejected his fuit ?"

" Neither."

" Not to reject, is to entertain."

" I deny the pofition, brother."

" Will you truft me with the true ftate of your own heart ?"

" Yes—

" Yes—with fincerity. As a proof of it, I own that of all mankind, my heart gives Wallace the preference."

My brother looked, Caroline, I know not how.

" I muft admire your candour, my fifter, how little foever I may approve your fentiments—for fuch a man—a man, mean enough to attack your purfe !"

" Brother—it is through my purfe he ftole into my heart. You labour under fome of my uncle's equivoques; but if you will be a patient auditor one half hour, you fhall hear all that has paffed amongft us; and your generous nature muft be much changed, if you do not approve the delicacy of Wallace's con-duct, howfoever you may diflike his affection."

I then gave my brother a very faithful account of *things*, amongft which, of Mr.

Wallace's

Wallace's gentility of manners, of his great good fenfe, of his exalted benevolence, of his birth, and of his misfortunes, " it was my hint to fpeak." — Having brought down this hiftory to the day of my departure for Kirkham, I concluded thus.

" So far, brother, there was not the leaft appearance on his part of any thing more than an extraordinary portion of duteous affiduity. For myfelf, my efteem was hourly on the increafe; but for love, it had never once entered my head; nor did I fufpect it, at my heart, till Mifs Thurl forced the fufpicion upon me, and a letter from my uncle, acquainting me of Mr. Wallace's danger, forced it ftill more. My uncle defired my immediate return. I obeyed, and found the malade reduced to a great excefs of weaknefs; the leaft motion almoft brought on a fainting. I confefs, brother, I could not fee him thus without pity; and I thought myfelf obliged to overlook fome little

discoveries

difcoveries which efcaped him — not in words—for to this hour he never prefumed to fpeak — but in fome little unguarded looks and actions, when the poor foul did not know what he was about.   It is true we took great care of him, both my aunt and I; and this not meeting the appro-bation of the good people in the kitchen, they animadverted upon it, and in due time fet half the tongues in Liverpool at work.   This reached Wallace's ear, I know not how, far before I knew any thing of it; and it determined him upon leaving England, which he did before he was well able to walk.   He wrote three letters, to my uncle, my aunt, and my-felf.   This is mine, the others I will procure you."

My brother read the letter, and even ftudied it; then owned, there was all ap-pearance of honour and delicacy on the part of Wallace; and on mine nothing that he could blame.   All he feared was, left my inclinations fhould be fo far en-gaged as to endanger my tranquillity.

" No,

" No, brother, anſwered I, not a tear ;
a ſigh, perhaps."

" Young ladies pique themſelves upon
fidelity in their firſt loves."

" Fear nothing from my romance, dear
brother : I could not promiſe where a
promiſe was never aſked ; nor am I ſo
little acquainted with the changeable nature of opinion as to burthen myſelf with
the faithful vow."

" I ſhould have been unhappy to have
my ſiſter, from the indulgence of ſome
fond idea, capable of rejecting eſtabliſh-
ments calculated to make her happy."

" Is this a general obſervation, brother,
or have you had the goodneſs to provide
for a beloved ſiſter ?"

" Not quite ſo ; but 1 would have her
ſee with an unclouded eye, and judge
with an unbiaſſed mind."

" Thank

" Thank you, brother."

" Sir Everard Moreton is dead.   After
a decent time my young friend has promifed me a vifit. It is not abfolutely
impoffible, but he may fee fomething in
my fifter which her brother fees."

" Is the picture a likenefs, which you
drew of him in your letters from Paris."

" A tolerable refemblance, as far as it
reaches."

" And could you recommend the original of fuch a picture to your fifter ?"

" Something, I hope, may be forgiven
to a young, rich, amorous, high-fpirited,
Englifhman of quality."

" I had rather not have the neceffity
of forgivenefs. My fyftem on this fubject, however, lies in little compafs. So
long as I think of Wallace, as I think of
                                    him

him now, so long as my heart tells me, it prefers him to every other man, no other man shall obtain me; but if your knight, or any other, can, by good and lawful means, transfer these feelings and sentiments to himself; and if such a man also should have your recommendation, dear brother, I think, I should pay a proper regard to it."

So, my dear Miss Thurl, ended this conversation; and so must end this letter, hoping that I shall very soon see you here, which, I assure you, I desire, even to longing.

In a few days my uncle quits this house for a pretty little country box, about half a mile off, giving up this house and the business to my brother. My aunt goes with my uncle, so that I am to be lady president here. Assure yourself I will be a kind hostess.

Yours,

JUDITH LAMOUNDE.

————————

MISS   EDWARDS,

T O

MISS   LAMOUNDE.

IF I had nothing more to plead, my dear Mifs Lamounde, than the common-pleas of carelefs correfpondents, for fuffering three of your letters to remain unanfwered, I fhould ill deferve your friendfhip or future regard; but Mr. Edwards, my excellent more than Father, has finifhed a long and painful ficknefs, by death. It is not a week fince he died in my arms, blefling me with his laft breath, and conjuring me to continue with my dear mother, and be her comfort and confolation, till Heaven pleafed to call her to a fimilar fate.

This folemn fcene of clofing mortality in my view, I have been able, indeed, to

weep

weep for your perplexities and diftreffes; but not to enjoy your livelier fcenes, comic as they are.

The effufions of fo fad a mind as I poffefs at prefent, may give you pain, but cannot give you pleafure. Indulge me, therefore, in filence a little time, and continue your friendfhip and correfpondence, which will be ever bleffings to your

PAULINA EDWARDS.

———

JAMES WALLACE,

T O

PARACELSUS HOLMAN.

On Board the Caithnefs at Sea.

I AM now preparing to relate to my friend, moft truly, all the circumftances which lately obtained me the honour of the world's notice, meaning

by the world, a fmall number of my
neighbours, as moft people mean.

It was my cuftom to rife with the fun,
that I might enjoy its earlieft and moft
chearing beams, and to walk a mile or
two into the country — moft commonly,
indeed, to a beautiful grove, a fhort mile
eaft of the town, the favourite walk of
Mifs Lamounde.

Entering this grove early one morning
in Auguft, I faw a bulky gentleman, by
his drefs a fea captain, fnoaring with great
emphafis amongft the trees. Not to difturb him, I turned my fteps to another
part of the grove. Prefently came in
ftaggering another fea captain, who fhook
the fleeping gentleman outrageoufly. —
" Devil burn ye now, my dear, fays he,
but get up, and when I've given you a
ball, you'll be after fleeping found enough."

The fat gentleman rubbed his eyes, and
as foon as he was able to difcern objects
                                    diftinctly,

diſtinctly, " The muckle deel gang awa wi ye doon Inverlochy, ſays he, for a loitering loon — Whare ha ye been, mon, theſe twa hoors ? Lig ye doon, mon, and ſleep aſpell."

" No, by Jaſus, ſays the other ; and I'll not ſleep in this world till I have ſent you into the next ; ſo riſe, and let's have a canonade."

" Gin you're in ſic muckle hurry to gang to the deel, tak your groond, mon, and fire awa."

After a few efforts the Scotſman roſe, and the Iriſhman reeling twenty paces back, fired his piſtol, the ball of which tore off the bark of a tree near the place where I ſtood, forty degrees at leaſt from the line of direction to his mark. The Scotſman ſtruck his piſtol, which miſſed fire. The Iriſhman fired again. His antagoniſt ſtruck his other piſtol, which miſſed fire alſo. Enraged at this, he

threw

threw it at the Hibernian's head, crying,
" Dom ye, mon, tak it aw together."

" By my fhoul, my dear, fays the Irifhman, drawing his hanger, we muft end
the combat with the fword."

The Scot drew his alfo, and ftaggered
to meet him ; but ftumbled over a ftump,
fell heavily down, and cut his leg with his
own hanger.

" And are you there, my dear ? cries
the Hibernian—and are you after dying
without being killed. By Jafus, now its
nothing but a trick to fave your life—but
it wont do ——."

The Irifhman was in earneft. He came
there to kill his antagonift, and thought
of nothing elfe. He raifed his arm to
ftrike, and, I believe, indeed, it would have
been the ftroke of fate to the poor Scot,
if I had not run at the inftant, and averted
the blow by a fmart rap with my walking-
                                                        cane

cane upon the Hibernian's elbow. The hanger fell from his hand, and, in ſtooping to recover it, he fell alſo.

" Gentlemen, ſays I, ſecuring both the weapons, you are my priſoners. I am a conſtable, bound to preſerve the King's peace."

" By Jaſus, ſays the Iriſhman, but I will ſqueeze your ſoul to tinder; do you know who you are talking to? A freeborn Iriſhman — and we have a King of our own, and a parliament too, honey; and the devil of any other law that we will ſubmit to at all at all."

" Hoot awa, mon, anſwers the Scot; ken ye what ye're gabbling aboot? Is not King George King of England and Ireland too ?"

" The devil burn the Iriſhman, anſwers the other, that cares who is King of England at all."

I 3   " If

" If, fays I, you were a fubject of the Grand Turk, you muft obey the laws of England whilft you are in it : So I muft beg the favour of you to go quietly to your quarters; and, when you have flept, I will do myfelf the honour to reftore your hangers, and, I hope, you will think no more of your difference."

" You fpake vary weel, fays the Scot; and, I believe, ye're a gude cheel that has faved one or twa of our lives. By Saint Andrew noo, captain Mac Nallin, punch and a whore ha been too many for baith oor wits. Come alang—and you froend (to me) weel gang too—for I'fe na part wi ye till I ken ye beetter—for dom the Scot that's bleend tull a kindnefs."

" Hear, you dog of a conftable, cries the Irifhman, would you be after leading Mac Nillan a prifoner from the field of battle ? Let Scotland yield to arbitrary power: I demand my arms."

" I

" I have no defire to offend, or offer
an infult, to any gentleman, anfwered I ;
I only wifh to keep the peace."

" That's aw reet," fays the Scot, taking
his hanger, and putting it in the fcab-
bard. The Hibernian did the fame, and
we fet out peaceably together towards the
town.

On the road I learnt that thefe two
combatants had been drinking all night,
and, inftead of going to bed, had agreed
to feek a nymph, had quarrelled about the
right of prior occupancy, had gone each
to his lodgings for piftols, which the Scotfman had forgot to load or prime, and had
appointed the grove to end the quarrel.

We had not advanced half way before
thefe gentlemen found themfelves deep
in politics, which they treated as drunken
people ufually do, with little fenfe, and
great intemperance of tongue. At length
they had recourfe to national afperfions,

I 4   which

which neither were in a temper to brook;
so, without more ceremony, out flew the
hangers, which I strove to beat down
with my cane. The affronted Irishman
turned his vengeance upon me, and gave
me a cut upon the left side with a hearty
good-will; for it went through my cloaths,
an inch deep into the flesh. Man never
thinks of two things at once. I thought
only of the savage brutality of the wound,
and not of the drunkenness which occa-
sioned it; and, in the extreme of anger,
struck him with my cane so forcibly upon
the right arm, that I broke it a little below the elbow. His weapon dropped:
I seized and threw it into the Mersey,
from which we were now not more than
thirty yards distant. The Scotchman
tossed his there also, crying, dom ye
baith—ye wull do na mair mischief in this
world.

Mac Nallin had reeled to a bank,
swearing revenge upon my damned con-
stableship; but captain Islay, that was
the

the Scotch gentleman's name, now faw
the blood ftreaming in great profufion
from my wound, and had fenfe enough
to fee the immediate neceffity of a furgeon: So taking me under the arm, we
went into the town, the captain endea-
vouring to perfuade me to be dreffed at
his lodgings.

But I thought I fhould die, my dear
Holman; and fhall I confefs my weaknefs, I longed to be pitied in dying by
Mifs Lamounde. The captain attended
me home therefore, and having delivered
me to the care of the coachman, the only
fervant up, he himfelf went to our moft
celebrated furgeon, returned with him,
and would not leave me till he had feen
my wound dreffed.

Before this bufinefs was finifhed Mr.
Lamounde was raifed, and came to my
room. He did not at firft fee the captain, and began afking me for reafons and
caufes, which pain not permitting me to

I 5 anfwer

anfwer inftantly, he began fuppofing, after his manner, that I had been raking all night, not ill-naturedly, but by way of triumph over my immaculate virtue — when the captain roared out—Hawd your gabble, Paul; ye fpeir nothing o'the bufinefs; the lad has been faving my life, and Mac Nallin's neck foa' a halter: For ye mun ken, after you left us laft night, Mac Nallin and I ftayed another bowl, and ane more: So when the punch had taken awa aw our underftanding, we quarrelled, and fteered to the grove, to kill one anaither, and this bra' lad preveented it, for which Mac Nallin had lik to ha' cut him doon: But the mon has got a broken arm; and faith I mun gang to take care of the fou, for he has no brains to luk tull himfell.

When the dreffing was finifhed, and the captain gone, Mr. Paul Lamounde kindly ordered me a very good apartment one pair of ftairs lower; and, indeed, had I been heir to the houfe, I could not have

had

had more indulgent treatment. Unfortunately an intermittent feized me, which delayed the cure of my wound, and brought me to an extremity of weaknefs.

It was a fortnight before I had the pleafure of feeing Mifs Lamounde, who was on a vifit at Kirkham; but, to make me amends, Madame Lamounde, the aunt, vifited me every day, and took fuch extraordinary pains about me, that the fervants began to talk. It is true, this lady had taken into her head the extraordinary fancy of being married, and had done me the honour to believe I fhould make her a loving hufband. As fhe is a lady of great decorum, it was an operation of three months, the communication of this fancy to me; and a very troublefome operation it was on both fides. I was obliged to put on the femblance of ftupidity; fhe to overftep the maidenbounds of modefty.

The

The innate benevolence of Miſs Lamounde brought her to ſee me as ſoon
as ſhe returned : I was not apprized of
her coming. Weak, both in body and
mind, it was too much for me : I had
nearly fallen from my chair ; ſhe ſup-
ported me. I opened my eyes, before
my ſenſes had fully recovered from their
trance, and did ſomething—I know not
what—for which ſhe chid me. I forbore
the guilt of words, and ſhe forgave.

But things were haſtening to a criſis.
William, the coachman, had the goodneſs to tell me how the people talked
about me and Madam, and how ſome
officious body had carried it to maſter.
This accounted for Mr. Lamounde's not
having called upon me for two or three
days paſt, and ſeemed to threaten me
with a diſagreeable *eclair-ciſſement*.

Miſs Lamounde, on the next viſit, ſaw
my ſpirits labouring with oppreſſion, and
had the goodneſs to ſympathiſe, and even
to

to difcover fome little marks of tendernefs. I prefumed to kifs her hand for
one expreffion of kindnefs, at the inftant
Sally entered, Madam Lamounde's maid.
Mifs Lamounde took leave, defiring me to
get well, and remember her advice. Sally
gave me a look peculiarly expreffive, that
feemed to fay, Oh!—fo it is—is it? I
preferved, however, a perfect compofure,
which laid Sally under the neceffity of
trying her own eloquence to bring me to
fhame.

"No wonder, Mr. Wallace, you holds
up your head above poor farvants, when
miftreffes condefcends to ———."

"To what, Mrs. Treffet?"

"Perhaps you may think that farvants
have neither eyes nor ears ; but, I affure
you, they have, and all their other fenfes,
as well as miftreffes."

"What

" What then, Mrs. Treffet ?"

" I don't fay that young men are to be blamed that goes about to mend their conditions ; for every body would mend their conditions if they could, and yet nobody can fay what will—and what wont ; for all's not gold that gliftens, and good wives aren't to be made of filks and fattens."

" I wifh, Mrs. Treffet, you would fpeak to be underftood."

" So I does—but nobody's fo blind as them that wont fee — and every body's apt to forget what they have been, when they gets above their fphere."

" You are above my underftanding, Mrs. Treffet : I wifh you would fpeak plain, or not at all."

" God help us—we was always proud enough—and fee how fnappifh we get."

" If

" If it gives you any pleasure to abuse me, Mrs. Treffet, you are kindly welcome; take your fill."

" Me abuse you, Mr. Wallace; me—that always takes your part—and that have tended you here day and night—but so it is to have to do with ungrateful people. All that poor sarvants do stands for nothing, when old mistresses, and young mistresses ——."

" I thank you for your care, Mrs. Treffet; but I wish you had less impertinence. What's the conduct of your mistresses to you?"

" What! when they behave ridiculously! Every body sees how ridiculous Madam has been ever since you have been ill; and, for aught I see, Miss is made of the same stuff."

" Hold your impertinent tongue, Mrs. Treffet, or walk out of the room. The

tongue

tongue that dares to calumniate your excellent young lady, ought to be plucked out for an example to evil fpeakers."

Mrs. Treffet turned pale with rage — " Don't go about for to fay that I caluminates my young lady, anfwered fhe, or my old lady either : I fcorn your words; but I know my own know. So, fince you be proud—take your own way – whereas I might have been a friend. Thank God, fome people arn't fo foon fet up as fome people. God help us — if pride was to govern us all !" Away went the meek and humble Sarah.

I laid myfelf down upon the couch : A multitude of indiftinct and rapid ideas crowded into my mind ; they agitated and wearied me. Unable to difentangle the chaos, or bear the tumult, I tried to fleep, and obtained at length a gentle flumber.

I was but juft rifen from the couch when captain Iflay called in. " My dear boy,

boy, fays he, I am glad to find you fo much better. That fneaking dog, Mac Nallin, has failed with malice in his heart againft you, for having prevented mifchief. I wull fail in fix days—but I canna gang wi true content, till I ha' been gratefu' to the lad who faved my lief."

" I beg you will not mention it, captain: It is a little fervice I fhall always refleét upon with pleafure."

" So wull I, my bra' cheel; but I wull think on't wi mare deleét, gin I'm allowed to reward it."

" And I with lefs."

Luk ye, fays he, I am captain Patrick Iflay, born and bred in the Highlands o' Scotland; one that never fuffers the loon that wrangs me to get awa' with impunity; nor the lad that ferves me withoot acknowledgement. Yefterday I dined at Wilfon's, the lawyer's, wha' fpeered into
the

the particulars of my foolifh bufinefs with
Mac Nallin. I hate a lie—fo I told the
hale truth. He faid a particular occafion
made him acquainted with ye; that he
did na ken hoo ye got into a fervant's
condition, probably by misfortune; for
that ye united the manners of a jontleman,
and the learning of a fcholar, with as honeft, as kind, and benevolent a heart, as
ever warmed a human bofom.

Noo, Wallace, withoot a lectel ambition, a young fellow is na worth a bawbee;
and it is na confonant to the nature o'things
for a chiel o'your erudition to ferve in fic
a poft. Gin you've any profpect by land,
I ha' three or four hundred poonds Englifh
ligging idle, and it is at your ferviée wi'
all my heart. Or gin you'll mak trial of
a feafaring life, gang the voyage with me:
The fhip and cargo are all my ain, boy.
Fifteen years I have ganged fra' port to
port, buying and felling, and doing what
I leek. When I am at fea I have books
and eafe—rather too much: But I grow

into

into years; the gout batters my carcafe,
and I want an underftanding freend, wi*
a heart o'kindnefs, to affociate with. I
ha' naither wife nor bairn, and ha' got
together a decent fpeel for age and infir-
mity. It may be, this fhall be my laft
voyage. Gin you wull bear a hand, I
promife you, upon the honour of a gentleman, ye wull ha' na occafion to repent
it."

"I know not, anfwered I, how I can
poffibly deferve your favours. My ignorance will render me ufelefs."

In anfwer to this, the captain informed
me his accounts fatigued him, and he had
more than once thought of taking out a
clerk; but what, fays he, is a mere clerk
to a confidential friend? He faid many
flattering things on this head, and I became really inclined to embrace his propofal; but Mifs Lamounde! Holman—
I had not the courage to determine to go,
although I faw, but too plainly, it was
improper

improper to ſtay. Thanking the captain, therefore, moſt ſincerely, I beg'd a
day or two to conſider of it, with which
he acquieſced, and for the preſent took
his leave.

But it was to no purpoſe to conſider,
when it was impoſſible to reſolve. Like
many other Chriſtian ſinners, I ſaw the right
path, but had too much weakneſs to over-
come the obſtructions that lay in the road
to it. Mrs. Treſſet had the goodneſs to
aſſiſt my determination. She came in the
evening to inform me that, though I had
uſed her very ill in the morning, ſhe
would ſhew me ſhe did not bear malice;
for to forget and to forgive was like a
Chriſtian. Then, in a tone at once que-
rulous and ſpiteful, ſhe told me what a
rumpus there was in the houſe. How
folks talked of Madam, and how Miſs
came in for her ſhare; how old maſter
had heard all about it; how he was ſullen
and glumpiſh, and never ſpoke to the
ladies all day. How Miſs pretended to
have

have the head-ach, and was gone crying to-bed. How it was all over Liverpool, and would be all over the whole world in a week; and finally, how foolifh it was to court out of one's own fphere.

"If, fays I, in a rage I was unable to fupprefs, if your innocent young miftrefs is talked of, it is owing to your lying and malignant tongue—and it is well for you, you are a woman. Had a man dared it— but go—go left I forget your fex, and treat you as you deferve."

"If ever I fpeak to you again, fays fhe, I'll be burned."

High as my anger was, it foon gave way to grief. Mifs Lamounde traducéd, and traduced for me! This injury, as far as poffible, I muft repair: There is but one way; I muft fee her no more: I muft not wait for explanations. I muft give the moft decifive proof that fhe is calumniated; and fure it is moft decifive to

go;

go; for who runs away from fortune and felicity, if there is any probable profpect of obtaining them.

This train of thought I continued till midnight; then rofe, and wrote three letters—one to Mifs Lamounde—the other to the uncle and aunt : They are not worth tranfcribing; you will guefs their purport. After I had finifhed thefe, I put all my worldly poffeffions into a trunk, and William, the coachman, being now up, I informed him I was difmiffed the evening before, and beg'd his affiftance to carry my trunk to a certain public-houfe upon the Dock, near which I knew the Caithnefs lay.

" Mafter Wallace, fays William, I'm forry you be going, damn me—if I an't; for, though you be proud, you be civil, and had rather do a body a good turn than an ill one."

When

When we arrived at the houfe, I treated William with a dram, gave him the letters, which he promifed to deliver faithfully, and then went on board the veffel to wait the captain's coming. He was furprifed to fee me, and received me with the greateft appearance of pleafure; affigned me a fmall cabin adjoining his own, and ordered the failors to treat me as himfelf.

We fet fail the third morning after, and I found myfelf greatly refrefhed by the fea breezes; indeed, I had grown ftronger ever fince I came on board. I was pleafed with every thing but the leaving Mifs Lamounde; and moft with that, whenever my heart would permit me to exult in the idea of having acted with a proper portion of honour and delicacy.

The captain and I fat down in the evening to our principal repaft, and feafoned it with felf-congratulation on the happinefs each propofed in the friendfhip

of

of the other. The captain facrificed at leaft a bottle upon the occafion, and fhewed me that he was a fenfible man, and joyous companion. "Maifter Wallace, fays he, ken ye what the worthy citizens of Liverpool are aboot? Raifing a ftatue to the memory of captain Iflay, for kidnapping a mon that froze auld mens hearts, and thawed auld womens. Antient virginity, they truft, may now reft fatisfied with cenforial dignity; and maiden affections return under the guidance of authority. Ken ye this terrible mon?"

I anfwered, no.

"They call him James Wallace, fays the captain."

I could not fupprefs the rifing figh, dear Holman, and begged the captain would fpare me upon that fubject.

"Weel, fays he, gin ye're fa delicate, Ife fay na mare. Love is na to be jefted
with,

with, lik a profane fubject ; but what wull I dee wi a letter directed to the faid James Wallace, which I got laft night fra' a Mifs Lamounde ?"

" Give it me, dear captain."

" When a mon renoonces the pomps and vanities o' this wicked world, he ought to flee temptation."

" Alas ! I have fled it."

The captain gave me the letter. I fend you copy. The dear original fhall never be out of my poffeffion.

When I had read my letter, fome dozen times, I afked the captain how he came by it ?"

" Ye mun know, fays he, that Paul Lamounde and I are intimate freends ; but we have cultivated that freendfhip moftly at taverns ; becaufe in private

VOL. II.   K   hoofes

hoofes one is fettered and plagued wi your domned politenefs; and, lik your Shenftone, I ay foond my warmeft welcome at an inn. I fupped with him laft night at the Talbot, and we ootftayed the reft of the company; when Paul himfelf gave me the letter, and defired his love to you, wifhed you a good voyage, and fhould be glad to hear of your welfare always.

I told him the motives which had induced me to wifh to carry you with me, and defired his opinion of you.

You muft have obferved, fays he, if ficknefs had not altered his features, that the fellow is " almoft damned in a fair face" — and to tell you a fecret which is fpreading apace all over this good town, both my fifter and my niece found it to their liking.

Now this is an accomplifhment no maifter of family would defire in a *male-*fervant, being apt to create confufion

amang

amang the females. The young man has moreover a found underftanding, and, I fuppofe, a large ftock of integrity. The fellow has damn'd fine fenfibilities too, and a nice notion of honour; but his greateft extravagance is a romantic benevolence; a folly of the firft magnitude, when there is nothing to fupport it. In fhort, the young man's qualities are all mifplaced. They would be damned good ornaments to accompany a ftar and garter.; but in a footman are ridiculous and outrè.

This inftant we are hailed by a homeward-bound veffel. I had much to fay of the captain's kindnefs and attention to me, and of my own tranquillity and eafe, one fubject excepted, of which, I think, too often; but muft make this up directly to accompany the captain's letters to England.

Dear Friend of my heart, adieu,

JAMES WALLACE."

MISS

————————

MISS LAMOUNDE,

T O

MISS EDWARDS.

Liverpool, March 20, 1788.

I HAVE your melancholy letter, my
dear Mifs Edwards, and am truly forry
for the occafion. The lofs of *fuch* a
friend muft be fenfibly felt by a grateful
heart, and yours is grateful. May I afk,
Paulina, if this lofs is aggravated by too
flender circumftances ? If fo, I claim the
deareft privilege of friendfhip.

It is now a month fince the veffel failed
which carried away the preceptor, who
taught me the proper ufe of fortune. To
you, Paulina, and Mifs Thurl, I own his
memory is moft dear to me, and I own
it without a blufh, for goodnefs gave
birth to the affection : Of him, therefore,
I can

I can write no more; to that Heaven, who infpires his virtues, I commit him.

I am not the only one who feels his lofs. My brother was fo pleafed with his character and behaviour at Abbeville, that he deftined him his confidential clerk ; to fay the truth, my dear, I believe, that he might purfue his own tafte for pleafure with greater confidence ; for I can perceive, by the effufions which efcape my brother, that he would be extremely glad to indulge in the pleafures of the metropolis.

" You talk," fays my uncle to him one day, when he had been expreffing his regret and the caufe of it—" You talk like a young man who trembles for his pleafures. I watched my clerks into honefty."

" I own, fays my brother, I had rather be fpared the trouble."

K 3   " Alas !

" Alas! poor young gentleman! You muſt, however, take the trouble, or the conſequences : But, without perpetual inſpection, no clerk, I think, is fit to be truſted."

" If there were, I preſume, you would allow Wallace to be one ?"

" Yes, anſwers my uncle, the young fellow ſeemed to me to have the vanity of integrity as much as any man."

" Vanity ! Sir !"

" Yes, fool—vanity. No man moves without a reaſon, nor *runs* without a paſſion."

" What is vanity, dear uncle ?"

" The itch, dear nephew, ſcratched by flattery ; and ſo obſtinate, the whole *materia medica* affords no ſpecific for its cure."

" This

" This is fatire, Sir, not definition."

" Well—I define it to be the univerfal caufe of all things done by man or woman."

" Good ! fays my brother; your moral metaphyfics lie in fmall compafs. Is ambition, is avarice, nothing ?"

" Not nothing—but begotten and born of vanity. Peep into thy own brain, thou wilt find her mounted upon the pineal gland; mark her fteps heedfully, you may trace her going to church."

Is my uncle logical in his conclufions, Paulina ? Do you recognize this active agent every where ?

Mifs Thurl had the goodnefs to pay me a vifit, almoft as foon as my uncle and aunt had retired to their country-houfe; and but for an accident that was very

K 4   likely

likely to happen, we fhould have paffed our days in tolerable tranquillity.

But to fee Mifs Thurl, and not to love her, proved to my brother an impoffible thing. She has beauty, wit, grace, and good-humour; twelve thoufand pounds left her by her aunt, and is the daughter of 'fquire Thurl, of Kirkham. All thefe qualities are fufficient to engage love, and fome of them to check prefumption. My brother, indeed, has good fenfe, fome eloquence, and a polite addrefs; but he has a fort of modefty, which fometimes proves an enemy to great undertakings; and this is the reafon, I fuppofe, why moft young gentlemen get rid of it as foon as poffible. He does not believe his perfon and merit to be fuch, that a young lady cannot fee him without being enamoured. He thinks too, that the all-accomplifhed Mifs Thurl muft look down upon a merchant; and, formed as fhe is to give dignity to rank, he confeffes, with a figh, it is almoft pity fhe fhould not.

I am

I am his confident, Paulina; to me he imparts his hopes, which are few, and his fears, which are without number. I am hers also, and know she does not despise my brother; though far enough, at present, from thinking of him, but as the brother of Miss Lamounde. I, for my part, will leave this delicate affair to its own progress; and will neither become the persecutor of my friend for the sake of my brother, nor will ever betray a sentiment to him, should she trust me with any, such excepted, as she herself might speak to him without impeachment of her delicacy.

Last Saturday night we spent three hours after supper, I believe, the most exquisitely pleasing my brother had ever known. My sweet friend was all herself, and supported her share of the conversation with such spirit, good sense, and sweetness; had displayed a succession of sentiments so void of pride, that my brother was convinced she must be uniformly

K 5   good

good and perfect, and that cruelty could
have no part in her compofition. This
comfortable conclufion he communicated
to me in the morning, and with it his
refolution to fpeak or die.

In the afternoon we were walking in
the garden, my brother thoughtful, and
bent upon the execution of his bold
defign, if he could any how get rid of
his fifter. Fortune favours the bold. A
fervant came; a gentleman defired to fee
me.

Then, as Mifs Thurl informs me, fhe
faw my brother's perturbations increafe.
She faw his eye fixed upon the alcove, as
if defirous to enter. She felt alfo his
trembling hand, and fufpected his fluttering heart : The wicked wantonnefs of
woman tempted her to fee how ridiculous
love could make a man of fenfe; fo fhe
walked compofedly into the alcove, and
took her feat.

My

My brother's tremulation was now greater than ever. He " looked as he would fpeak," but no found iffued from his lips. At length he took the fair lady by the hand, and, having communicated to it a part of its own paralitic affection, he raifed his timid eyes to hers—and faid— Madam—Mifs Thurl—I hope—I humbly hope ——.

It was not Mifs Thurl's bufinefs you know to comply with hopes before they were expreffed; fo, withdrawing her hand gently from his, and pointing to a fantaftical ornament in a neighbouring garden, enquired what it was.

My brother did not hear the queftion; he only felt the hand withdrawn, and the fhock in confequence; fo anfwered the enquiry thus: " The prefumption, Madam—I own the prefumption—but your goodnefs, Mifs Thurl — When you confider the perfect refpect—almoft to adoration—you will not punifh that prefumption as it deferves ——."

K 6

My

My brother was now growing bolder and more confiftent, when I had the misfortune, in my turn, to be the ill-omened bird of interruption, by intro-ducing Sir Antony Havelley.

Oh, dear! fays Mifs Thurl, rifing to meet him—my coufin."

Sir Antony faluted her with infinite grace, and was then introduced to my brother, to whom he faid, with an air of dignity—the brother of Mifs Lamounde, Sir, muft be a gentleman of infinite merit and confequence; and I fhall efteem this a moft aufpicious hour, if it fhall prove to be the firft dawn of a friendfhip that is to end with life. James, confidering the late perturbation of his mind, fucceeded pretty well, I think, in his anfwer.

Sir Antony, fays he, cannot offer friend-fhip without conferring a favour. Not to accept it with infinite refpect, would de-

clare

clare me void of common fenfe as well
as politenefs.

A great many fine fpeeches were made
on both fides, which are not, I believe, to
be found in the academy of compliments;
and then we entered into general converfation, in which we had not been long
engaged before it was interrupted by a
well-known voice, faying, no—no—friend
—I'll go to her—never mind ceremony—
and the door opening, entered Mr. Havelley Thurl, in dirty boots, a common
riding frock, and in all points the reverfe
of the elegant, and brilliantly habited, Sir
Antony Havelley.

The 'fquire was performing his beft
honours to the ladies, when Sir Antony
caught his eye, and arrefted at once his
legs, and his elocution. He opened his
mouth to take a more affured view, and,
having fatisfied himfelf as to the goodnefs of his optics—" Hey—coufin, Sir
Antony, fays he, be you here?"

Sir Antony affumed an air of dignity, and was filent. "Well, fays the 'fquire, if that's your humour keep it, and much good may it do you. For my part, I never bears no ill-will to nobody, when the heat's over."

"Nor Sir Antony neither, I dare fay, brother, anfwers Mifs Thurl."

"Now there you're out, fifter, for he's as fulky as fin — And he goes in cold blood, and writes me a challenge to go and fight him, fword and piftol, beyond fea, among the papifhes : But I writes him word back I did not like on't—for why ? If I'd been killed, Jack Cornbury faid, I could not ha' got Chriftian burial. So I offered, d' ye fee—to have a bout at boxing or cudgels, and then be friends— for why fhould relations go for to kill one another ?—And from that day to this he never fends me a word of anfwer."

"Mr.

" Mr. Havelley Thurl, fays the baronet, you have not had the education of a
gentleman, nor I, of a ploughman; therefore it is not probable we fhould come to
a right underftanding concerning any one
thing in life."

" That's as much as to fay, fays the
'fquire, that I'm no better than a ploughman, and I cod that's better than a monkey or a civet cat."

" Brute—brute—fays the baronet—I
defpife thee."

" Brute—brute—returns the 'fquire—
By jigs—1 wifh I had thee upo' Kirkham—
Moor—I'd foon fhew thee whether I was
a man or no."

" Brother, fays Mifs Thurl, before you
came we were quiet."

" Why you may be quiet ftill, fays the
'fquire; it's coufin, Sir Antony I be angry

at,

at, not you, nor Mifs Lamounde, nor this gentleman here as I don't know."

" This gentleman, fays Mifs Thurl, is Mr. Lamounde, Mifs Lamounde's brother."

" Sarvant, Sir, fays the 'fquire. I hope you don't take it amifs 'at I talk to coufin, Sir Antony, here in your houfe as it were, becaufe, mayhap, he's your gueft; for, mayhap, he comes courting Mifs here."

" I hope, replies my brother, I fhall never have occafion to take any thing amifs, either of Sir Antony or you, Mr. Thurl: I am forry you have had any caufe of quarrel, and wifh I might afpire to the honour of reconciling you."

" Never mind, fays the 'fquire, pulling my brother by the fleeve, to ftop him whilft Sir Antony and the ladies walked to the houfe. Never mind—it's as well as it is. I'll bet you a guinea now you don't don't guefs what coufin, Sir Antony, and I differed about."

" About the beft hunter, or the beft pointer, perhaps, replied my brother."

" Lord love you, fays the 'fquire, you be a mile off. Why, coufin, Sir Antony, never hunts nothing but butterflies, and it's my belief he daren't let a gun off; for I offered to fight him wi' fowling pieces, and I cod he was right to be off; for, though I fay it that fhould not fay it, I am one of the beft fhots in Lancafhire; but as to coufin, Sir Antony, it's my belief, he's not half a man. What do you think I did? I ftole into his dreffing-room one day, and I'll be hanged if he had not more pill boxes, and patch boxes, and gewgaws, than your fifter and mine both together!"

" Very likely, anfwers my brother; he feems a nice gentleman; but, as he came

in

in not an hour ago, and I never faw him before, I know little of him."

"No! fays the 'fquire—Why I thought he'd come a courting to Mifs."

"That may be his errand, anfwers my brother; but this is the firft time he ever came hither."

"Is it by your truly, now?"

"It is, indeed, and, I think, he might have faved himfelf the trouble; for, if I know any thing of my fifter, he will not be to her tafte."

"By George! fays the 'fquire, then I have a good mind to have another touch at her; for d'ye fee, I was her fweetheart firft, at a ball here, and I fhould ha' courted her yet, if fhe had not fcorned me: But no matter—let her have her own way—If fhe takes coufin, Sir Antony here, may-hap, fhe'll ha' the worft on it. What, **though**

though he be a bit taller and flimmer
than I be, fee how folid I be put together.
As to coufin, Sir Antony, you may blow
through him. If I did not fhake all his
bones out of joint at three fhakes, I'd ha'
nothing for my pains ; but I ben't of a
humour to die for love. If I takes a
fancy to a young woman, I tells her fo ;
if fhe likes on't, well and good ; if not,
there's others that will, and what fignifies
fretting."

" I muft own, fays my brother, I think
your fyftem of love-making very rational."

" Yes, anfwers the 'fquire, I think it
be. By George, you'll find I don't want
fenfe, when we come to be better acquainted ; and I defire you'll come and take a
fortnight's fhooting with me next September : I'll fhew you fport. For what,
though your fifter does not fancy me —
that's no reafon why we fhould not be
friends, is it ?"

" No,

" No, certainly, fays my brother ; and, I affure you, your acquaintance will give me great pleafure, for I take you to be an honeft, hearty, good, Fnglifh country gentleman, which is a very refpectable character."

" Give me your hand, fays the 'fquire ; you be as fenfible as a judge, and I fhould like to crack a bottle wi you."

" Do me the honour then to take a bed with me to night."

" Why I fhould like it hugely, but not if coufin, Sir Antony, ftays ; for then we fhould be jawing like mad."

" He'll not ftay without invitation, certainly ; and, though I chufe to be civil to every gentleman, there are fome I fhould not like to be intimate with."

" Then I'll ftay, fays the 'fquire ; but let's crack a bottle after fupper, for I've got fomething to tell you."

My

My brother having agreed to the proposal, they followed the ladies, and found, to the 'fquire's great fatisfaction, Sir Antony had taken his leave. This polite gentleman begged a thoufand pardons for the invincible neceffity under which he lay, of denying himfelf the exquifite pleafure of drinking tea, with the ladies that afternoon; but hoped he might be permitted to repay himfelf on the morrow.

We fat down to tea, and Mifs Thurl began to reprove her brother for his rudenefs and incivility to Sir Antony.

"There's it now, fays the 'fquire, it's all my fault. Coufin, Sir Antony's not a bit rude, if he calls me a hundred names. Did not he tell me I was a ploughman and a brute? By George, I'd ha' bruted him if you had not been by: I'd ha' laced his fine French jacket."

" A hundred years ago, brother, thefe manners might have been fupportable; but

but where do you hear now of gentlemen beating one another ?"

" As if killing one another was not as bad as beating; but women are always taken in by the eye. If so be a gentleman wears fine cloaths, and makes fine speeches, that's all in all with them; though, mayhap, he may have no more honefty and free-heartednefs than will fill a thimble."

" It is very poffible, brother, to unite good qualities with agreeable ones; and, to make fociety happy, no man ought to be permitted to treat another uncivilly before company. Above all things, it is moft ungenteel and unmannerly to begin a quarrel before ladies: He who does fo, is either fuppofed to be a coward, whom every body will infult, or a tyrant, whom every body will fhun."

" Ha' you done, fifter? Blood, ha' you done ?"

" Every

" Every body knows, brother, you have good natural fenfe; but for want of good company ――."

" Like coufin, Sir Antony's—ha ?"

" No, brother; he has too many refinements, and you too few. To make a gentleman, you fhould meet half way."

" I'll tell you what, fifter; rather than be like coufin, Sir Antony, in any one thing in this world, I'd be a pig."

" I muft own, fays my brother, I think, if Mr. Thurl fhould meet Sir Antony half way, he would be a lofer by the bargain. I allow, indeed, that Mr. Thurl's exterior manners are not fo polifhed as the prefent age requires; but Mifs Thurl will be fo good to remember, that, under an exterior much more unpolifhed, our anceftors had to boaft of a manlinefs of action, and a generofity of fpirit and fentiment, which, I fear, are incompatible
with

with the refinements Sir Antony feems to have adopted. If I enter into Mr. Thurl's character right, the true bafis of it is honour and honefty. His temper, indeed, feems hafty, and his language rather incorrect; but time will foften the one, and improve the other, efpecially by the aid of good company and books."

"There now, fifter, fays the 'fquire, here's Mr. Lamounde has faid more to th' purpofe in a minute, than you'd ha' preached in an hour. If he finds fault with one thing, he gi's a body one's due in another. You be for nothing but fault finding."

"You are miftaken, brother; I know you have many good qualities—that you are friendly and generous—and that you had rather do a good action than a mean one."

"You talks now fomething to the purpofe, fays the 'fquire; and if you'd bid

me

me keep Mr. Lamounde company, inſtead of couſin, Sir Antony, I'd ha' minded what you ſaid—for, though I ſpeak it be-fore his face, he has more ſenſe in his little finger, than couſin, Sir Antony, has in all his body."

This converſation ended with a very amicable convention; that Mr. Thurl ſhould read, when it did not make his head ach, and keep my brother company as much as he could when ſhooting and hunting ſeaſons were over.

At eleven, Miſs Thurl and I retired, and then the 'ſquire inſiſted upon his bar-gain. It was not, I believe, much to my brother's taſte; but all things are poſſible to a man who has love in his heart, and deſign in his head.

The beſt way to pleaſe a man inclined to talk, is to liſten; and my brother liſ-tened, or ſeemed to liſten very profound-ly, the ſpace of two bottles, in which the

'ſquire

'fquire fhone extremely; and was fo pleafed with my brother's attention and complaifance, and fo elevated by found old port, that he pulled his chair nearer my brother, and, with a lowered voice, and an air of more than common importance, afked him, " How he liked his fifter ?"

My brother anfwered, he thought her the moſt amiable young lady he had ever feen.

" You fhall have her, fays the 'fquire; mind what I fay. Father told me one day, as if fhe married to pleafe him and me, he'd make her up twenty thoufand. Now I know I can bring him about, tho' you ben't a landed man; and, as to Mother, what I fays, is law; but then one good turn deferves another: I like your fifter. What, though fhe can't fancy me yet, mayhap fhe may, when I gets polite, as you're to teach me, you know; but then I won't learn too much on't, for

I hates

I hates your soft-spoken gentlemen wi
voices like bull-rushes when wind blows
among 'em, grinning e'ery mouthful of
words they put out, to make believe
they're better humoured than other folk.
Now I'd rather be as I be than so, for, I
think, it's all unnatural; for why can't a
man speak wi's own voice, and look wi'
face that God has gi'n him. Come—
push bottle — I be dry. Now, sister,
mayhap, thinks as I want to learn to
talk—but there she's out—I can talk fast
enough, and to purpose, though I say it
that should not say it — but be like my
words don't all come out pop in grammar order—for though I learnt a pretty
bit o'latin, I never could make much
o'grammar: And Father would no' send
me to school—so parson taught me—and
I kept company most an end with Kirkham farmers, and good fellows too, for
matter o'that; and wi' Father's huntsmen
and grooms, and so I learnt some o'their
lingo—for that's but natural. Come, fill
glasses — here's to better acquaintance.

I'm

I'm as glad I gotten you for a friend, al. moft as if any body had g'en me a hundred a year; if fo be my fifter can but fancy you, and your fifter can fancy me, I fhall be proud on you for a brother, as if you'd been a gentleman born: And why fhouldn't they? You be handfome enough, and I be a proper perfon too; none o'your fpindle-legged chaps, like coufin, Sir Antony. Well now—I'll tell you a fecret; but be fure don't tell on't again, for fear Father fhould hear; the laffes of our town are ready to run mad o'me. At this precious minute o'time there's two on 'em wi' child, and I'm at my wits end to know what to do with them; but come—hob and nob—I never thinks on 'em but they make me dry. Now you muft not tell your fifter o'this, becaufe fome women make but little account of a man that meddles wi' any but themfelves. No more fhan't I, when we be married; but it's better to fow all one's wild oats aforehand, int'it now? A body may always take up when one's a mind, mayn't

mayn't they ? Now I be heir to five
thoufand acres of as good land as ever
crow flew over. It's true it's underlet —
but that's Father fault – not mine : It
can be raifed, can't it, when time ferves ?
By George, brother Lamounde, you
flinches your glafs, I think. You ben't
a milk fop, be you ? Come—a man never
knows a man to th' bottom till he's made
him drunk. Here's a brimmer to our
laffes. Come, I'll gi' thee a fentiment :
Wine to our women, and women to our
wine. In't it a good one ? I'd a mind to
make a fong once, when Moll Parkins
was coy and froppifh.

If you wou'd know a piece o' my mind,
I love's a lafs that's coming and kind :

But, by George, afore I could think o'th'
next line, Moll yielded, and fo there was
no occafion for't you fee. Now I'll tell
thee a good joke : When Moll and I had
been gracious together like, fhe took airs,
and nothing would ferve but neighbours
muft call her miftrefs ; for Moll would

L 3   be

be miftrefs, and miftrefs would be madam, and madam my lady. All that's natural to women — and that makes me think o' being a baronet when Father dies. May-hap it may take wi' your fifter, though fhe told me no when I courted her firft; but, I believe, that was only out o' fpite."

This, my dear Paulina, my brother gave me as a fmall fpecimen of the 'fquire's elocution this memorable night. At length the 'fquire could fpeak no longer, and fell afleep. My brother con-figned him over to Scipio and another fervant, who got him to-bed. Whilft they undreffed him, he opened his eyes once or twice, growled out a few prayers, as they thought, and faid fomething about the devil.

My brother rofe in the morning with an aching head, and made a great many ferious reflections upon drunkennefs, and his new brother; and concluded, that all
                                        things

things muſt be endured for love, as well as faith.

When he came into the breakfaſt-parlour, he found the 'ſquire taking his firſt draught from a large tankard of October with a toaſt. Here, ſays the 'ſquire, ſhaking him by the hand—take a ſwig— it will ſettle your head—My brother deſired to be excuſed—I tell you, ſays the 'ſquire, you need not be afraid on't, it's mild as milk — Why, my hand ſhakes like an aſpin ſometimes of a morning—I takes a pull or two, and it's as ſteady as a tree. Still my brother perſiſting in his refuſal, the 'ſquire, to ſhew him his folly, pulled it to the bottom.

Miſs Thurl and I entered. So, brother, ſays ſhe, at your uſual morning exerciſe ; you will certainly injure yourſelf by it.

There you be out, ſiſter, ſays the 'ſquire; it's hearty and nouriſhing, and

L 4   gi's

gi's a body fpirits, efpecially when one has had a fup too much o'er night.

I hope, fays Mifs Thurl, you did not keep Mr. Lamounde up drinking?

A bit fifter, anfwers the 'fquire; for feeing as he and I got into a liking for one another, I was not minded to go to-bed wi dry lips; fo one bottle brought on another, and I got a little deep: Now every body has fancies o' one fort or other, drunk or fober; and, would you think it, I got a notion the devil un-dreffed me, and put me to-bed, and it was the firft thing I thought at this morning, fo it made me a little low like, and fo I took a whet—and, by George, if the la-dies, with their ratafees and cordial waters, would take a little more to found ale — it would ——.

Scipio's entrance cut fhort the fentence, and arrefted the 'fquire's eyes. After a minute's paufe, he afked my brother, in

a

a low voice, if that was his fervant?
Yes, anfwered my brother, and the very
devil that laft night flew away with you
to-bed.

By George — I'm as glad on't as ever
was — for when I came to think about
it this morning, it put me in mind of the
Catechifm and Ten Commandments, and,
by the Lord, I could remember nothing
o' them: And then—as I'd been a little
wicked wi wenches you know—how could
I tell what the devil might have to fay
to me—but I'm glad there's nothing in't.
When you come a fhooting—I'll take
you to fee **Moll Parkins**—a fine crummy
wench. If you like her—but mum.

After breakfaft my brother was beginning to entertain Mifs Thurl with a little
hiftory of Scipio, who has, indeed, great
claim upon the kindnefs of our family;
for he once faved my Father's life, and
was capable of acting in an extraordinary
manner upon a certain occafion, relative

to

to himfelf. My brother had fcarce begun this ftory, when — " God blefs my foul fays the 'fquire, I was fo fluftered with coufin, Sir Antony, yefterday, and toffi- cated wi' one thing or other all night, that I quite forgot to tell you what I came about. Mother fent me to wifh you to come home as to-day, and were to ha' fent chaife this morning, if fo be I had gotten back laft night.

" Is any thing the matter, brother ?"

" Not 'at fignifies much, only fhe's a bit out of order."

" Oh, dear ! how unpardonable this is, brother? Shall I beg the favour of Mr. Lamounde to fend to order the Tal- bot chaife directly."

" Why, fifter—Women are always in fuch a flurry, when there's no occafion. Dr. Rundle was fent for — fo you fee there's no danger ; only Mother's whee-
zing's

zing's got bad again. One may hear her
down into th' blue parlour."

" Lord have mercy! fays Mifs Thurl.
I never was fo angry at you, brother, in
my life."

" Clap a plaifter o'th' angry place,
fifter. What! a body can't always remember when they will."

Nothing, my dear Paulina, could have
happened fo *mal-a-propos* as Mifs Thurl's
departure; for it left me alone, expofed
to all the fury of Sir Antony Havelby's
courtfhip. I received the baronet in the
afternoon, with a full determination to
put a final period to his addreffes; but
I was not fo happy. The baronet, en-
trenched in compliments and forms, was
not able to arrive at the declaration he
meditated in lefs than a full hour, and
my brother arrived before its completion.
The remainder of the vifit paffed moftly
in fcientific converfation, in which Sir

L 6   Antony

Antony fhone, or thought he fhone, ex-tremely; and went away perfectly fatisfied that he had gained the admiration, and confequently the efteem, of Mr. La-mounde.

This is a long letter, my dear Paulina; it is probable it may weary you as much to read, as me to write. I will give you a refpite — and only tell you I am always

Yours,

JUDITH LAMOUNDE.

—————

JAMES WALLACE,

TO

PARACELSUS HOLMAN.

The Caithnefs.

THAT my friend ftill lives in my remembrance, what better proof can I give than taking every opportunity

my

my duty will permit, of conversing with him in the only possible manner that distance allows. But what, dear Holman, can be my subject? The sea, as sea, you know better than myself. The elements. of plain-sailing would be useless. Of love, you would have more than enough; yet, if I spoke from the abundance of my heart, it is of love only I should speak.

It happens very fortunately that captain Iflay, by way of table conversation, has, at different times, given me a kind of abstract of his life, and, on my asking leave to make it the subject of my letters to you, he permitted it most willingly. This abstract methodized, I am now going to entertain you with, as near as my memory will allow, *in his own words*, for it is of importance to me, that the esteem he has already conceived for you should be mutual.

" Sir

" Sir Wallace Iſlay, my Father, was the laird of a ſma' clan, in the county of Caithneſs, and did aw he could to ſupport the anſient greatneſs of our hooſe ; for he had four bag-pipers that piped him in and out, waked him at early dawn, and ſang him to reſt at dewy eve.

" My Father married a bonny High-land laſſie, with an immenſe fortune in richneſs of blude. Her talents were vary great. Seventeen of her offspring were aw alive at once ; but it pleaſed the fates only three ſons, and as many daughters, grew up to maturity ; and even theſe contributed mare to the venerability of our Sire, than to his felicity.

" Save and except about one hundred acres of land, in the neighbourhood o' Cromartie, aw the territory of our antient hooſe, which ſpread itſelf over moors and mountains round aboot the caſtle of Loth-gairn, were barely ſufficient to ſupport its dignity. Ye may gar at its fertility when

ye

ye ken, that not aboon 'one twentieth found other confumers than the laird and his clan; confequently, as ye may weel expect, Sir Wallace had little filler, and lefs gold.

" My Maither was a gude wife—but fhe was a woman—and a woman, according to Virgil, is an animal delighting in finery. The Cromartie acres produced the fole revenue that could be exchanged for articles of tafte and fafhion, and they were too few by half.

" All the clan thought my Father a great mon; great upon the hills; great in the hall; great every where but in his ain parlour He loft authority by contention, and contention was there inevitable and for ay. Sell thofe dirty lands at Cromartie, and dinna let thefe bonny chiels difgrace their noble blude. This was the fang o'the parlour, and this was the chorus.

" At

" At length Sir Wallace yielded. The land was fold. One part of the purchafe was deftined to fit out my elder braither Archibald, and buy him an honourable place in the metropolis; another to purchafe a commiffion for Wallace, my fecond braither, in fome Scotch or Englifh regiment; the third was fet afide for my fifters fortunes; and the fourth for prefent elegance. As to poor Patrick, he was na mare confidered in this treaty of convention, than if poor Patrick had na' been born. This was the reafon.

" Notwithftanding the richnefs of my Maither's blude, the purity of it had been fullied by one degenerate branch of the family. This was a younger braither of her Faither, who chanced to be fmitten forely with the charms of a burgher's daughter of Cromartie. He took the maid to wife, a crime of great magnitude; he fucceeded in due time to all the burgher's money, which was ample, and

to

to his traffic alfo. The whole conftituted
an unpardonable enormity.

" This merchant had a fon who fucceeded his Father, and proved as gude a
chiel as could fpring fra' fic a contami-
nated ftock. He had the difcretion to
give his aunt and female coufins, at Lothgaim, fome deft pieces of India manu-
facture, for the ornament of their proper
perfons; and my Father had the generofity to overlook the fou 'ftain, and acknowledge him for a relation.

" This gentleman, whofe name was
Lochiel, took a liking to me, and obtained permiffion to carry me home, on
condition of giving me an education fuitable to my blude. So I learned latin
and mathematics, and read hiftory auld
and new : But with aw my learning, I
I naver could ken how exchanging the
goods of one nation for thofe of another,
and benefiting baith by the operation,
could damage my blude.

" I

" I was with this relation when the grand convention was made, and the proverb, out of fight, out of mind, was verified in my favour. My elder braither got a poft at Edinburgh, which fuited him weel; for it brought fome filler, little employment, and na contamination of dignity. My younger braither, a bonny bra' lad as e'er ganged the mountains o'Lothgaim, had a commiffion in an Englifh regiment. He fell in love with a Mifs Corbet, of Lincolnfhire, for his heart was as tender as valiant; got her gang with him to Kirk, and the next year was ordered to Germany.

" But firft he implored Sir Wallace's pardon, in a vary humble letter, in which he pourtrayed his wife's gude qualifications. At the fame time he informed him that the match was na liked by the girl's Father and Maither, wha would na' be reconciled. Sir Wallace chafed lik a wounded boar, when he learned that the mon wha made fo little eftimation of the

beft

beſt blude in the eaſtern Highlands, was
na mare than an Engliſh parſon.

" My poor braither obtained leave to
throw himſelf at his Father's feet in perſon, hoping to find an aſylum for his wife;
but aw in vain: Sir Wallace would na
ſee him. I was the only perſon of our
famıly wha took the leaſt notice of him,
and I did it at my peril. Lochiel, however, invited him to Cromartie, whence
I returned with him to the borders, and
ſaw his wife. She was a lovely woman,
and big with child. We parted with true
tears. He departed for Germany, and
ſhe after him, as we ſuppoſe, as ſoon as
ſhe was lighted. The poor lad was killed
in battle, and of her we never heard more.
She was a lovely woman, and he as bra'
a lad as ever ganged the mountains o'
Lothgaim.

" Our next family occurrence was the
marriage of my elder braither to a lady
of Clydeſdale, a widow, wha had ſix hun-

dred

dred pounds sterling per annum, and a
hoose in Edinburg. She was a lady of
great politeness, wha never said a rude
thing, except to her inferiors. She had
the complaisance to pay a visit of duty to
Lothgaim, to express her satisfaction at
every thing she saw there, and to invite
my Father, Maither, and Sisters, to the
metropolis.

"But a journey to the capital could
na' be underta'en without muckle siller,
and Sir Wallace did na' possess twelve
ounces. As the thing, however, was in-
dispensible, he was under the necessity of
granting a mortgage for four hundred
pounds to cousin Lochiel, of Cromartie.
With this sum they made an appearance
suitable to the renoon of our lineage.
Alas! in twelve months, it had melted lik
snaw in the valley; and the pair of elders
ran back teell their mountains, where
alone they could be oot o' danger, and
defy the world, the flesh, and the deel.
My sisters remained at Edinburg.

"What

" What might be the proximate caufe
—I dinna ken—for Lothgaim is na lefs
remarkable for the longevity of its inha-
bitants than other Highland clans — but
my Father and Maither, though far fhort
of an hundred, fickened baith at once,
and died the following winter. On this
occafion I was fent for hame, and had the
fatisfaction to ha' the hale affliction to
myfell.

" Sir Archibald, however, arrived alone
in time for the funeral rites; and the will
being opened in due form, the new hede
of the houfe found himfell burdened with
a legacy of one thoufand pounds to me,
and five hundred pounds to each of my
fifters, payable in the year, and was left
to raife it how he could.

" He ca'd to his aid a mon o' fkill,
wha' had, moreover, gude common fenfe
and humanity. This gentleman fet a
progreffional value upon the lands — at
firft a low one — and rifing yearly till it
reached

reached the apex — for, fays he, your tenants have a market to create — they have alfo a higher degree of fkill and induftry to acquire — and they muft have time for aw.

" This was a raifonable propofition; my braither could find nathing to object to it, but his ain needs; fo, having difmiffed the mon o' fcience, he ordered a new rent role to be difperfed amang his clan, commuting aw for filler, and beginning at the top of the valuation inftede of the bottom.

" The clamour was loud and grievous; the baronet could na ftand it : So, affuring me I was the beft o' braithers, and that my welfare fhould be ay his care and delect, he conjured me to ftay at Lothgaim, and mak the beft hond I could o' the baifts. Furthermore, that I fhould live at his expence, and ftint myfell in nathing that could give me content. For his part, his poft required his prefence in the metropolis,

metropolis, and he felt muckle impatience to be in the arms of his dear wife. He might have added—and in thofe of a young Lowland laffie, whom he indulged in a quiet retreat in Clydefdale, and whom he loved quite as weel; but this circumftance I did na then ken.

"This poft of fteward I accepted with muckle reluctance, and kept it one year. If Lothgaim were to be my reward, I fhould na fpend fic another; it produced much tumult, and little filler. I pleafed nobody, not even myfell. The clan complained of my oppreffion; the baronet of my confcience. The din was loud about me, and the poft, inftede of comfort, brought me na but reproof. Between them I loft my patience; fo gathering my accoonts together, I carried them to Edinburg, and threw them, with fome refentment, at my braither's feet He difputed every article, and the fum of fifty-five pounds, my year's fubfiftence, he called enormous. Injurious reproaches
rendered

rendered the feud between us almoſt dedely; and we parted with aw the rancour of—braithers.

"As to my incomparable ſiſters, no dare creatures could have made greater improvment in leſs time. Three years before, with hunting poles in their hands, and their coats tucked up to the knee, lik their godeſs Diana's, they would have ſprung after the hounds over the ſtony encloſures that divide our demeſnes. Already had they learned not to be able to walk — to mince and fritter the broad Highland eloquence into infantine liſpings —to languiſh with nervous affections — with other poleetneſſes, which mingled with their Highland manners, like oil and water. The ſweet girls were incenſed beyond meaſure, that I ſhould take the part of the Highland brutes againſt Sir Archibald, laird of the clan, and my elder braither.

"My

" My illuftrious blude was all in a fer-
ment with the treatment I had met with ;
and I returned to Cromartie with muckle
fpleen, and meditating vengeance. Coufin Lochiel received me kindly, for he
loved me weel : He had alfo his caufes
of complaint ; fo, after a formal demand
of the money due to each of us, we began to batter the baronet with the red-hot
balls of law.

" But this was lik to be a work of
time ; and I had an immediate call upon
me for action on anaither account, which
I muft gang back to trace to its fource.

" You are an aftronomer, and ken the
length o' winter nights in a latitude of 58°,
and you may weel enough conjecture the
comforts of an auld caftle, inhabited by
three people, and fometimes half buried
in fnow. The three indwellers were, myfell, a lad of fifteen, my groom, and footman, and a Highland laffie of twenty-four,
with black eyne, fair red legs, and higs of

a delicate fandy brightnefs.   The Highland maidens are mare remarkable for dirt
than beauty ; but Mauge, as fhe 'was
handfome, had the vanity of being clean ; fo
that when een came on, when fhe had
donned her ftockings, and fmoothened her
cockernoony, fhe was an object of muckle
charms.   It is true, Pliny Livy, Maclau-
rin and Sympfon, amufed me weel; but
they tired me too, and I looked at the
beauteous Mauge for pure recreation.
Mare finful thoughts came at length into
my hede ; for what can be more finful
than to rob a poor girl of her chaftity.
The deel fhall ha' me before I'll doot,
fays I ; and this refolution I ftrengthened
by a volume of fermons, which fpit fire
and flame againft fornication both fimple
and complex; and I ha' no doubt I fhould
ha' gained a decided victory, gin I had
been blind.   In a long conteft, the flefh
and the deel are ay too powerful.

" When I quitted Lothgaim for Edinburg, poor Mauge had the misfortune to
                                                    be

be pregnant. When I returned, the Kirk had got hold of her, and were perfecuting the poor laffie, *pro falute animæ*, with the fame Calviniftic clemency that burnt Servetus. The paftor of Lothgaim happened to be a man of great learning in things of Heaven ; but vary little underftanding in things human, of great bigotry, and fma' humanity. I knew he was malignant, and believed him hypocritical. When a youth, I had dared to laugh at the whites of his eyne turned Heavenward, at his long graces, and puritannic cant. He prophefied that I would be a fon of Satan, and hated me with all the piety of a prieft.

" The prophecy had now become true, and Mefs Andrew could na lofe fo bra' an opportunity of exultation and revenge. He preached with fic a divine fervor, that aw the parifhioners were convinced I was the deel's ain chiel, and were willing to affift the paftor in executing heavenly juftice cn fic an abandoned mifcreant. He

M 2

drew up a memorial, and got it figned by aw who could write, and marked with the fymbol of a crofs by aw who could not.

" This memorial was tranfmitted to Sir Archibald, wha pioufly anfwered, Heaven forbid he fhould fcreen a delinquent, tho' his ain braither. Nay, een for the love he bare me, he defired I might tafte the falutary chaftifement of Heaven, inflicted by its haly minifters, for the gude baith of my foul and body.

" But before the haly minifter directed the fpiritual thunderbolt againft my breaft, he chofe that Mauge fhould have the be-nefit of it. After fundry leffer penances, and terrifying the poor girl with the fplen-did difplay of hell torments, they were upon the point of expofing her to public fhame in a white fheet, in the parifh-church of Lothgaim.

" This I could na brook. I have aw proper refpect for religion, but none for

its

its grimace; nor could I bear that the
spiritual gang should invade the province
of the civil magistrate, and punish, not in
proportion to the injury done to society,
but the injury done to God's holy ordi-
nances, of which they have the manufac-
ture and the direction.

"Mauge was still my servant as weel
as the lad; baith lived in the castle at my
expence; nor was I yet cast out fra' my
stewardship. Accompanied by my cousin
Lochiel, I repaired to Lothgaim, and
found my poor girl terribly at a loss,
whether to look on me with kindness or
horror. They had endeavoured to per-
suade her, her precious soul would be lost,
gin she did na shun me, as she would the
great deel himsell Whilst the pastor was
thundering out his terrible admonitions,
Mauge believed and trembled. When he
was gone she found her heart refractory.
My coming decided the conteest, and
earthly affections triumphed over heavenly,
as they usually do.

"I

" It was dark when we arrived at Loth-gaim ; and, as our intention was to abate the paftor's haly zeal for perfecution, we kept our coming fecret ; and the next Sabbath, being the day of penance, we fent Mauge off by moon-light to Cromartie, in the care of Lochiel's fervant, and fpent the remaining time in fettling our plan.

" In order that fo meritorious a work fhould ha' the greateft number of fpectators poffible, the gude paftor had given a month's notice, that it fhould be performed that Sabbath in the afternoon, and Mauge was ordered to attend. The hour came, but Mauge did na', which the paftor attributing to fear and fhame, fent four gude matrons to bring her, as we had forefeen ; one of them proved to be our boy's mother, a cafe we had provided for.

" The lad preinftructed, and faithful as a Scot, met the matrons with his hair unkembed, with muckle diforder in his

drefs,

drefs, and mare in his looks; and, running
to them, Oh, maither! maither! fays he,
I weel gang hame wi ye; I'd na lig another neet ith caftle for aw Cromartie town.
Sic yellings and yelpings. I fhrunk hede
and ears into my bed, and darft na pop my
eyne not till noon. Eer fince I ha' been
upo' th' gang high and low aw o'er the
caftie for Mauge; and I fears as how the
muckle deel lugged her awa ith neet.

" Oh! thank my gude St. Andrew,
for preferving my bairn, my dear bairn,
fays the Maither, clinging about his neck..
Then withoot mare enquiry, they trotted
back to the paftor, where Jockey told his
tale with its needful appendages; for nature had given the chiel a gude memory,
and we ftored it weel with matter. The
paftor, though prone to fuperftition, its
follies, and its fears, had in this cafe wifdom enough to fufpect a trick; fo he hied
back to the caftle with Jock and the women, threatening the poor boy aw the

way

way with God's anger and his air, if he had ony hand in't.

" Jockey affirmed his innocence, and to mak it mare manifeft, was active in leading the fearch thro' the caftle, in opening doors, and peeping into clofets ; but always pulling his Maither alang with him. When they approached the end of a long gallery, Jockey's terrors, at the fight of a door which fronted it, greatly increafed. He trembled much, and drawing his Maither back — for loo o' Chrift, fays he, dinna let our paftor gang in there; th' auld laird walks there aw in white. A mon 'f God, fays the paftor, frays not at fpirits—Jock—open the door. Na, anfwers Jockey, na for the wide world. Hoot awa Tike, fays the paftor. I ken ye noo. I fpeer weel enough wha the ghaift is ; fo faying, he pufhed at the door, which yielded to his haly touch, and difcovered a figure, indeed, aw in white, ftalking across the far end of the room, which had na mare light than was admitted at the door.

door. The women fhrieked, and fell upon their knees. The paftor, advancing boldly, cries oot, I fpeer it aw. Mauge—the wrath of Gode wul fall heavily on you for this profanation. He had fcarce ended the denunciation, when the floor opened a hideous chafm, and the poor paftor funk into the bowels of the earth. The door fhut with a clap that echoed through the caftle; the lightening flafhed in their faces, and the thunder rolled above. Jockey ran off: The poor fouls hobbled after as faft as they could get; and, withoot turning back to fee if the great deel was behind, gained the church-yard withoot lofs o' life or limb.

" It would be wafte of words to defcribe the confufion there. In this hale clan, there was na one prefumptuous infidel wha dared to doubt. All believed, and all were terrified.

" A grey-headed carle, a mon o' fecond fight, gathered an audience in one

corner.

corner. Freends, fays he, it is na for
nought that mairning vifions come to
Sawney Garblocken. I awoke at dawn
of day, and I faid, Rife Sawney, and
gang thee to Lothgaim. Then, faid I,
for what? Thou art thy fell a mon o
frailty, Sawney Garblocken; why deleeteft
thou in feeing a frail fifter brought to
fhame? Gin the gude Gode had dealt
with thee as the paftor o' Lothgaim deals
with weak maidens, whrt would have become o' thee, Sawney Garblocken? So I
would nae gang; and fmoothering my
pillow, compofed myfell for a wee bit mare
o' fleep. Behold, freends! a figure came
wi aw the lineaments o' the paftor o'
Lothgaim, and faid unto me, Gin thou
beeft a mon o' Chreeft, gang thy gait to
Lothgaim, Sawney Garblocken; fo I
donned my garb, and followed the mon
o' Gode, wha fpake not till he came to the
rock o' Dronnold, and the rock o' Dron-
-nold opened, and I faw the mon o' Gode
na mare! Then was I carried back a-
gain to my bed by fome power invifible,
                                    and

and my body flowed wi moifture! Freends!
I could reft na mare: I rofe, and came
alang to Lothgaim.

"Whilft aw was waiting in the church-
yard, the poor paftor lay half fmoothered
upon a bed of feathers; for ye mun ken
the haunted chamber was direeƈtly over
the feather hoofe in a corner o' the caftle.
I believe I need not be minute in my
explication; ye may ha' a fhrewd guefs
the hale contrivance. Lochiel, and Jock,
and I, cut the boards: I was the ghaift
aw in white. I flafhed the powder when
the paftor was fwallowed up. Lochiel,
when he ken'd the lightening's glare,
rolled the thunder upon the leads of the
caftle. The drama was now near its clofe.

"We did na defire to keep the paftor
long in his dark apartment, left fome o'
the church-yard guefts, wifer or bolder
than the reft, fhould propofe a vifit to
the caftle: So, after we had fuffered him
to pray and groan a while, I ca'd to him

M 6   with

with a voice mare than human, for it was
conveyed through a hunter's horn—Andrew—rife—I am thy gude angel. At
my interceſſion thy ſins are forgiven. Aſ-
ſume na mare the power of Heaven to
chaſtiſe a ſiſter—leſs a ſinner than thyſell;
for, under the pretence of zeal, thou haſt
indulged in rancour, malice, and revenge.
Repent, and go thy way; an angel guides
thee.

" At this inſtant Andrew ſaw a thin
column of light: He groped his way to-
ward it, and, to his muckle joy, found
it proceed from a ſma' opening of a door
which led into the court-yard o' the caſtle.
His gude angel lifted him alang, ſo that
he flew rather than walked, till he reeſted
his weary leegs ſafe upo' conſecrated
ground.

" His flock gathered round him with
increaſed reverence; the proper due of a
haly man returned fra' the ſhades below,
in hopes to hear what was doing there;
but

but the paftor only told them, he had feen
fic things as neer were feen by mortal
eyne; and that, on the next Sabbath, gin
he might be permitted to reveal the fecrets o' the other world, they fhould hear
aw, and he would pray to Gode to gi'
them comprehenfion; for they were things
far beyond the ordinary pooers of the human underftanding. So, difmiffing aw
wi his bleffing, he withdrew to his ain
hoofe to ponder upo' the marvels o' the
nether world.

"We left the caftle the fame night, and
the faithfu' Jockey, wha' is ftill my fervant, joined us in a few days. Mauge
was. fafely delivered, but the child died.
We na mare repeated our fins, and Mauge
was foon after weel married. The tale
o' the haunted room was carried to the
baronet at Edinburg, wha fpeered the
hale wi' muckle fagacity, and took no
fma' pains to bring us to condign punifhment for fic flagrant behaviour to a
minifter o' the Kirk; but the haly purpofe

pofe was defeated for want of evidence:
Lochiel and I had better fuccefs; we
recovered aw we fued for wi' cofts.

" It was under the advice and direction
o' this worthy relation I commenced merchant and navigator. I have followed
the bufinefs twenty years with grete glee,
and fome fuccefs. I ha' got a fpeel for
auld age, and having na hairs, for my
braither has na legitimate children, and
my fifters never knew the bleffings o'
matrimony, I ha' made my will in favour
of coufin Lochiel, wha is a bacheleor too,
and has paid me the fame compliment.
I have remembered fome auld friends,
and fhall add a claufe in remembrance of,
at leaft one, new one."

We are entering the Tagus, dear Holman. A bufy fcene is opening before
me, to which I muft attend. Farewell,
dear friend—I will feize the firft opportunity to fend this, and give you frefh news
of your

JAMES WALLACE.

MISS LAMOUNDI,

T O.

MISS EDWARDS.

Liverpool.

I DO excuſe you, my dear Paulina, as you deſired me in your ſhort billet; and moſt ſincerely do I wiſh, the viſit of Sir Everard Moreton may be attended with all poſſible happineſs to my ſweet friend, and the worthy relict of the excellent Mr. Edwards. It was certainly a generous letter he wrote Mrs. Edwards, and will, I hope, be followed by correſpondent action: But, Paulina — there have been known in this world — nay, even in England—young gentlemen, amorous, plauſible and deſigning. You will ſcarcely believe it, my dear — but the cloak of generoſity has ſometimes been worn to hide a very bad ſhape. Sir Everard

rard Moreton may, for aught I know, have all the virtues that dignify the gentleman — but alfo, he may not. He is not now, Paulina, the ingenuous youth at fchool. He has been at Paris, Paulina— a bad fchool to teach a lover fidelity. Thefe infinuations, my dear, are plainly defigned to caution you. This is an age in which a young woman cannot well put too little confidence in flatteries, in promifes, efpecially of young, rich, titled gentlemen, who have feen the world and Paris, with the eyes it is ufually feen with at twenty-one. Be cautious, therefore, dear Paulina, and forgive the impertinence of my friendfhip, for daring to infinuate the neceffity of it. I will now proceed to your requeft, and continue the hiftory of the loves of Antony Havelby and Judith Lamounde.

You muft have perceived the baronet's head to be full of elegance, etiquette, and virtu'. I fuppofe he conceived, that as I had permitted him to fee me twice at

my

my own houfe without a frown, and that
my brother had feemed pleafed with the
brilliancy of his talents, his merit muft
be irrefiftible; and that the amour was
brought precifely to that degree of ad-
vancement, that rendered it proper to
announce his pretenfions to the heads of
the family.

The morning after the interview, I
mentioned in my laft, he ordered his cha-
riot to the houfe of Paul Lamounde, Efq;
and, fending in his name, was fhewn into
the parlour, where my aunt attended him
as foon as the proper change could be
made in fundry parts of her habiliment.

My uncle, though no connoiffeur, had
a tafte for the extraordinaries of nature,
and his mercantile connexions had enabled
him to form a fmall collection. Amongft
other things that now adorned the parlour,
was a piece of Bolognian ftone, which,
having been much fpeculated upon whilft
Sir Antony was in Italy, the many things
he

he had heard of it, rushed into his mind so forcibly, that they drove out of it Miss Lamounde, his love, his business, and all his elegant attentions.

My aunt already stood beside him, had thrown away her first honours, and, before the baronet was disengaged, my uncle entered also. Brother, says my aunt, Sir Antony Havelby.

I am Sir Antony's most obedient, answered my uncle.

Sir Antony heard them distinctly, and made a very elegant, and, I suppose, instinctive bow. Sir, says he, this is the Bolognian stone; probably you know its property of shining in the dark—but it has other properties which may not have come to your knowledge.

Was it to communicate these, says my uncle, that Sir Antony did me the honour to call upon me to-day?

The

The baronet recollected himself, and might blush for aught I know, could the blush have been seen. I request your pardon, good Sir, says he, I perceive my abstraction has led me into a strange error in point of politeness; and I request yours also, Madam. I shall be overwhelmed with confusion, if you believe me capable of failing in the moft profound refpect and efteem for the ladies, the dear objects from whom we extract felicity.

Humph! fays my uncle—I fhould be glad to know the procefs.

The baronet, whofe recovery was now compleat, fmiled, and went on. I have taken the liberty to wait upon this lady and you this morning, Mr. Lamounde, in order to lay a propofal of a very delicate nature before you. It is my ambition, Sir, to act in all cafes like a gentleman, and man of honour; nor is the attempt to fteal into any family clandeftinely confiftent with my rank or fortune.

I

I prefume to fay, that fome fplendid fami-
lies have courted my alliance, and, confidering the honours which have been
beftowed upon me, for I affure you, Mr.
Lamounde, I am fellow, *fpeciali gratia*,
of no lefs than three foreign academies
of fcience, as alfo of our illuftrious royal
fociety at home :—To which I muft add—.

The propofal itfelf, anfwered my uncle,
which, amongft fo many illuftrious con-
fiderations, may, I fear, chance to be forgot.

Now this was not very polite, Paulina ;
but my uncle does not value himfelf
upon this quality : However, it was not
the baronet's bufinefs to be captious ; fo,
though, I fuppofe fomething mortified,
he continued his oration.

I hope, Mr. Lamounde, you will not
think my exordium fuperfluous, when you
confider I come here a candidate for fa-
your, and therefore ought to offer fome
reafons

reasons why I may hope to merit the favour I solicit. Your good-will, Sir, and this lady's, may, for what I know, be essential, even to my existence; for my suite, Mr. Lamounde, is of that delicate nature, that may require the aid of collateral love and friendship. A cloud upon your brow, Sir, or upon this lady's, may overcast the dawn of my chearful day; the fair enslaver of my heart ——.

Oh! a love suit then—says my uncle. If it would not be giving you too much trouble, Sir Antony, I should be glad to know the lady's name.

If my heart was laid open to your inspection, Sir, you might read it there; for there it is wrote in characters indelible. She is a lady, Sir, whose beauty is her least perfection; whose praises were I to expatiate upon as they deserve, the day would be too short.

Humph!

Humph! says my uncle; I thought a name had lain in a smaller compass. She is not Spanish, I hope.

A small matter of offence appeared in the baronet's countenance. My penetrating aunt saw it, and said—My brother is always cross, Sir Antony, when he hears women praised; but he is very fond of his niece, and ready to hear proposals for her benefit.

Good !—Beck—says my uncle—this *is* coming to the point: Is my niece then, Sir Antony, the fair enslaver of your heart?

To see and not adore her, replies Sir Antony, would denote me blind to the perfection of female merit.

And what do you desire of me, Sir Antony? asked my uncle.

Your permission, Sir, and your interest, says Sir Antony.

Neither

Neither of which, anfwers my uncle, are worth a ftraw. Young ladies now acknowledge no authority in matters of love, but the heart. Befides, Sir Antony, fhe has eyes, and a good common under-ftanding, and, I dare fay, will be able to chufe herfelf a hufband. My fifter here may, perhaps, think more highly of her own influence, and it is impoffible fhe fhould refufe it to fo accomplifhed a gen-tleman. To her I beg leave to refer you, Sir Antony, and wifh you—a good-morrow.

With infinite pleafure I accept the re-ference, faid Sir Antony, as foon as my uncle had withdrawn : I can expect no-thing but what is polite, courteous, and obliging, from a lady, to whom, I am perfuaded, Mifs Lamounde is indebted for a large portion of perfonal and mental grace.

So fublime a compliment, perhaps, had never reached the ears of my aunt, even

in

in her moſt blooming days.   How could
ſhe anſwer it otherwiſe than with the ut-
moſt courteſy.   " She was ſenſible the
alliance of ſo ſuperior a gentleman muſt
do them honour , and ſhe hoped ſhe ſtood
upon ſuch terms with the niece, that,
ſhe ſhould be able to promote it."

Sir Antony anſwered, he ſhould be indebted to her for more than life : So, after
a few more compliments and precautions,
he kiſſed her fair hand, and took his
leave.

My uncle, who truly loves me, poſted
up to our houſe, to enquire concerning
this phænomenon.   " I ſuppoſe, ſays he,
you expeſt I ſhould thank you now, for
the compliment you paid me this morning ?"

" I ought not to let any day paſs without ſome mark of my duty and affeſtion
to a very croſs good uncle ; but I have
no peculiar claim to-day."

                                        " You

" You fent me Sir Antony Havelby. Where did you pick him up ?"

" At Kirkham."

" He's of a new order of coxcombs. I have never feen any before who joined foppery to fcience."

" I am told the conjunction is common at Paris."

" And this is the firft importation. Prithee, Judith, which of his fine qualities art thou captivated with ?"

" Women, dear uncle, feldom fall in love with learning ; but Sir Antony, as you muft needs fee, has a charming tafte in drefs ; then you cannot but remark how genteel he is."

" Yes—if it be ungenteel to have a carcafe of flefh and blood."

Vol. II. N " Then

" Then his penfive gentleman like air, uncle.—And his title ; is it for the daughter of a fimple merchant to refift fo many attractions ?"

Humph! fays my uncle. I wifh I could fpell my uncle's Humph, Paulina, provided it could be fpelt ; but it is nothing more than the letter M pronounced with the mouth fhut.

" Befides, continued I, he is virtuofo and connoiffeur. His collection of fhells and pictures will be the admiration of the whole county. Then he has the honour to be abftracted, uncle; a fure fign how very profound he is."

M—fays my uncle ; fhut your mouth, Paulina.

" So, my dear Sir, fays I, you really fet him down for a coxcomb ?"

" He

" He did not imprefs me with much veneration. When he has the honour of being your hufband, I fuppofe I fhall fee him with other eyes."

" But I have the misfortune to think him a coxcomb, dear uncle, as well as you ; and he cannot have the honour of being your nephew, until I have experienced a great revolution of fentiment."

" Why doft keep him dangling after thee then ? But a woman never can prevail upon herfelf to difmifs a lover, whether bear or monkey."

" I have not had opportunity, Sir ; he has not yet honoured me with a declaration. Yefterday he was in labour of it a full hour. I had the greateft reafon in the world to expeft his delivery, when my brother came in, and Sir Antony's pains went off in fcientific effufions."

N 2   My

My uncle told me he was glad I was not fuch a damned fool as the generality of my fex; then giving me a kind kifs, departed.

About five in the evening came Sir Antony, with increafed confequence, I thought, and increafed gravity. I received him alone, and was fo very gracious, that in fifteen minutes he told me he had that morning taken the liberty to wait upon Mr. and Mrs. Lamounde, and hoped he left them propitious to his wifhes.

" Was it upon my account you gave yourfelf that trouble, Sir Antony ?"

" Certainly, Mifs Lamounde; can you doubt it ?"

" I am forry, Sir Antony, you did not think me of fufficient confequence to be informed of this intention : I could, perhaps,

haps, have convinced you there was not the leaft neceffity for it."

" Although you are perfectly independent, my dear Mifs Lamounde, I hope you will confider it as a proper decorum in me."

" At leaft, Sir Antony, it was extremely premature, unlefs you fuppofed it impoffible I fhould find any thing to objeft, whenever you chofe to do me the honour to declare your fentiments."

" I muft own, Mifs Lamounde, I had prefumed to flatter myfelf that there could arife no objeftion of confequence. Could it be to my birth, my rank, my fortune ?"

" To none of thefe, Sir Antony."

" I hope I may fay without vanity, Mifs Lamounde, that my underftanding is not contemptible; and for my perfon,

N 3   I muft

I muſt own it would be *toute nouvelle* to find it was become the averſion of the ladies."

" I have no deſire to controvert theſe ſentiments, Sir Antony; but I am not diſpoſed to marry."

" I flatter myſelf fate may have deſtined me to be the happy man, that is to create this diſpoſition."

" I don't ſee the probability, Sir."

" This is very mortifying, Miſs Lamounde : Will you do me the favour to mention in what particulars I have the misfortune to be diſagreeable to you ?"

" Diſagreeable ! Sir Antony. This is your language, not mine. Sure I may be allowed to decline the honour you intend me, without ſuch an inference."

" Excuſe

"Excuse the timidity of a lover, Miss Lamounde; I fear I have a rival—a favoured rival."

"If so, Sir Antony, I presume it will be a sufficient reason why you should desist from your intention."

"I would not, Miss Lamounde, credit the voice of fame, where it depreciates a lady."

"Speak plainly, Sir Antony."

"The subject is so immensely delicate, Madam, that I cannot—upon my honour—as I cannot give it credit—so I find it impossible to give it language."

"Your delicacy, Sir Antony, is extreme. My footman, I suppose."

"Name the horrid idea no more, dear Madam. It is not possible the accomplished Miss Lamounde could stoop to

N 4   such

fuch an object. It is not poffible fhe
fhould treat Sir Antony Havelby with fo
much indignity, as to give him fuch a
rival ; a rival with whom he could not
meafure his fword ; a rival who would be
honoured by his cane ———."

" I allow the fublimity of thefe ideas,
Sir Antony; but muft beg leave to in-
terrupt their courfe, in order to rectify an
error into which you have fallen, by fuppofing the accomplifhed Mifs Lamounde
muft be blind to merit, becaufe it has.
neither title, nor coat of the loom of
Lyons. That I may not caft another indignity upon Sir Antony Havelby, by
fuffering the greatnefs of his own conceptions to lead him into miftake, I think
myfelf bound in honour to acquaint him,
that I *bad* a footman for whom I entertained a very fincere regard, and upon
whom, as in all appearance Sir Antony
would chufe to pay a prudent regard to
his own perfon, I would not have him
confer the honour of his cane."

Sir

Sir Antony rofe from his feat with great dignity.—" I am forry, Madam—I am in defpair — I wifh you all imaginable felicity—but you have the cruelty to excite a civil war betwixt my honour and my love."

" I beg leave to end the conteft in favour of honour; for love would only perfift in an unavailing fuit."

" Unavailing! Mifs Lamounde; and have I then the mortification of entering the lifts againft a valet, and of lofing the day?"

" If you chufe to mortify yourfelf with imaginary caufes—Sir Antony ——."

" Imaginary! dear Mifs Lamounde— Say only, you have no prediletion for that fellow —I beg pardon, dear Madam; but fay this only — you revive my hopes— you reftore me again to life."

" Pardon

" Pardon me — Sir Antony. Exclu-
five of my near relations, I have not yet
feen any man, for whom I have conceived
fo great an efteem, regard, or, if you will,
predilection, as for that fellow."

" Mifs Lamounde — I wifh you all poffible happinefs — but after fuch an avowal,
I own it is not with Sir Antony Havelby
you can expect it."

" It is not with Sir Antony Havelby I
do expect it."

" Madam, I take a moft reluctant leave."

" Sir Antony, your humble fervant."

So ends, my dear Paulina, the hiftory of
the loves of Antony Havelby and

JUDITH LAMOUNDE.

I have a letter from Mifs Thurl — a fad
one. The lives of both her parents are
precarious ; her Mother's hangs by a
thread.

CAPTAIN

_____

CAPTAIN ISLAY,

T O

PAUL LAMOUNDE, ESQ.

Lifbon.

Dear Paul,

THERE was kindnefs in your private defire, that I would write you
about James Wallace, and I fulfil it with
pleafure. It was well for me that you did
not know the true value of what fortune
had thrown in your way, otherwife, inftead
of being my right-hand at Lifbon, he
would have been yours in the accompting-
houfe at Liverpool. Genius, you know,
Paul, carries improvement wherefoever
it carries application; and James, in the
great leading points of failing, is a better
feaman than myfelf. He found amongft
my old books a Spanifh Grammar and

N 6   Dictionary,

Dictionary, with Don Quixote and Friar Gerund, and in fix weeks he read them both. He is much careffed by our gentlemen of the factory here, and very advantageous terms have been offered him. Once I perfuaded him to accept them; he burft into tears, and anfwered, if I was indifferent to him, he was indifferent to life; for having no profpect of pleafure but in my friendfhip, that loft, all was loft. Paul, I hugged the bra' lad in my arms, and fwore, that nothing but death would part us.

But, fays I, do you defign to forget your Judith Lamounde ?

No—never—never. Though the remembrance afflicts me — it is dear and facred, anfwered he; but it is perfectly without hope, and confequently without expectation.

That's right, no doubt, fays I; for I fuppofe that furly old fool, Paul, looks up to grandeur for his niece.

James

James ſtopt—and for the firſt time gave me a look that ſeemed to indicate diſpleaſure.

Captain Iſlay, ſays he, you tell me your acquaintance with Mr. Lamounde is of old ſtanding How is it poſſible you could apply to him, an epithet ſo harſh and ſo improper ?

Is not that the epithet, ſays I, that all lovers apply to fathers and uncles, who croſs their fond wiſhes ?

" The language of paſſion, Sir, is always unjuſt."

" The whole town of Liverpool admit the epithet, ſurly, as his proper due."

" Mr. Paul Lamounde reſembles a pine-apple. He has a rough outſide, but beautiful even in roughneſs His interior has every thing in it that recommends man to man."

How

How like you your advocate, Paul? But no matter, for the boy is mine now, and I shall have the making of him.

I have disposed of my cargo, and taken in half lading for Algiers. I have three or four honest Muffulmen to take leave of before we depart for our respective paradises. From thence I will go to Valencia, where I have friends I will like to see once more, and there, perhaps, take in my *last* cargo. As I pass the Streights, I will land Wallace at Gibraltar, and send him by land to Valencia, to settle some old accounts, and prepare new purchases.

Old friend, farewell. The time, I hope, is coming when you and I will have nothing more to do than drink our old mens milk together.

PATRICK ISLAY.

————————

MISS   EDWARDS,

T O

MISS   LAMOUNDE.

Box.

I CANNOT exprefs my obligations to my kind friend for the trouble fhe has taken to amufe me, when I moft wanted amufement; and for the friendly cautions in her laft favour, when, perhaps, I moft want caution.

Yet I hope not. Though my fluttering heart confeffes its conquerer, Sir Everard Moreton has hitherto given me no caufe to fufpect a change in his own. My dear Mrs. Edwards almoft doats upon him, he is fo polite, fo attentive, and fo generous. To me, his language is all tendernefs; his eyes—oh—if they are but the faithful interpreters of his heart. And why fhould
they

they not, my dear Miſs Lamounde ? Why
ſhould an ingenuous mind ruſh upon
ſuſpicion, when there appears no cauſe to
excite it ? Sure it is but common juſtice
to give a perſon credit for good intention,
till he has ſhewn himſelf diſpoſed to bad.

I know I am his inferior ; but ſome
minds delight in conferring obligations.
Why ſhould not his be one ? I am ſure
if I was a queen, the moſt delightful act
of majeſty would be to make the man I
loved a king.

Sir Everard has not taken up his reſi-
dence in our houſe, nor even in our vil-
lage, but at an inn two miles hence. Is
not this extremely conſiderate, my dear
Miſs Lamounde ? And does it not ſhew
a delicacy one would hardly expect from
ſo young a man ? But, indeed, my dear,
you can ſcarce conceive how very delicate
he is. I dare ſay it is owing to that, that
he has not yet ſpoke to me in direct terms
of marriage ; for that would have been
very

very precipitate you know, confidering the recent deaths of his Father and mine.

He does not talk of quitting his prefent fituation, till he can prevail upon my dear Mrs. Edwards to honour him with her company to a pleafant country feat in Weftmoreland. Is not this a confirmation of his honourable intentions? It is true, the feafon is not favourable for excurfion; but one may be equally happy within doors as without, in company one likes.

It is now near the hour Sir Everard ufually comes, fo that I am fure my dear Mifs Lamounde will excufe my writing more, and continue the bleffings of her friendfhip and correfpondence to her poor

PAULINA EDWARDS.

SIR EVERARD MORETON,

T O

JAMES LAMOUNDE, ESQ.

Tarbix.

FAITH, Lamounde—I have no other apology to make, for not being with you at the time appointed, but that my charmer grows every day more charming. Let the belles of Paris and of London boaft their refinements and their ton, I grant them the power to animate fometimes; but the flood of foft and tender fenfations, fuch as my Paulina knows to give, is not theirs to beftow. It is from humble, from domeftic life, where alone fenfibility can grow into a habit, thofe foft, engaging fweetneffes muft come, which have the power to captivate a heart like mine.

But,

But, Lamounde – to make a wife of this divine little girl, to raife her into rank, to introduce her to the *belle monde*—would be to deftroy the hen that laid me the golden eggs of felicity. No faith – I am not fuch an idiot: It is one thing to marry; it is another thing to love. Marriage is a facrament, a divine, folemn, legal, and fpiritual bufinefs. Love is not fpiritual—but volatile as air. Does he not fpread his light wings and fly at fight of folemnities ? Then catch him again, if you can.

I have learnt wifdom, Lamounde; how fhould I not, fo precep'd as you know I was for nine long months. If my honoured Father were now alive, I would marry to pleafe him : As he is not, I will marry to pleafe my Mother; for, after all, parents are ufually pretty clear-fighted as to the folid requifites that make the marriage ftate happy, and my Mother has already glanced at a girl of a million. — After this, will any cafuift prieft deny my

right

right to love? A wife, Lamounde, for affairs of ftate; but for affairs, not of ftate, a maid—a maid.

Not that I dare hint a fyllable of this to my charmer. Her virtuous fpirit would fly out of its prifon at the bare mention of it. She is fo abundantly ftocked with maxims of piety, that all the arts of per-fuafion would be tried in vain. No—fhe muft be furprized into it: I have almoft per-fuaded that credulous old woman, her re-puted Mother—for by the by, my Paulina dropt into her lap — out of the moon, I believe—having no Father or Mother in this world — But this is too long a tale— I fay I have almoft perfuaded her to go with me into Weftmoreland And then— adieu, Lamounde! Pray for my fuccefs.

Yours,

EVERARD MORETON.

JAMES

———————

JAMES LAMOUNDE, ESQ.

T O

SIR EVERARD MORETON.

Liverpool.

I CONJURE you, my dear Sir Everard, by every thing facred—by the awful names of religion and virtue—by all the ties of humanity — and all the laws that refpect the peace of fociety—for all will be infringed—I conjure you, give up the enterprize you have conceived.

Ill fhould I deferve the name of friend, could I fuffer the paffions of the man it is my boaft to call by that name, to plunge him into irretrievable guilt, and entail upon him a bitter and lafting compunction, without an endeavour to fave him.

You are the head, Sir Everard, of an antient houfe; you have its honours to
maintain,

maintain, and tranfmit to a *legitimate* pof-
terity. Is it Sir Everard Moreton who is
ftooping to the fraud, the deception of in-
trigue ? Is it he who will do to a woman,
what common integrity will not permit
to be done to a man ?

It is your own acknowledgement, my
friend, that perfuafion would be vain ; and
fure perfuafion ought to be the ultimate
boundary, even of a libertine ; beyond,
is infamy.

Every word you utter in the praife of
your *divine* Paulina, is to your own condemnation. Is it for the lovelieft of women to infpire only illicit defire ? Is it
becaufe fhe is poor and unfriended ? Becaufe fhe is an orphan ? Becaufe fhe has
a fuperior claim to the compaffion of every
breaft indued with humanity, that you
would degrade her to the duft ?

By Heaven ! Sir Everard, I am agitated
almoft to frenzy, when I think of fo much
excellence,

excellence, fuch fweet fimplicity, as you have defcribed; for I know her not, devoted — nay trepanned into involuntary ignominy. I ftop my pen, left I fay fomething too rude for friendfhip. I am always, dear Moreton, and never more than at this inftant,

Your Friend,

JAMES LAMOUNDE.

END OF THE SECOND VOLUME.